As the Crow Flies

by Ron Pruitt

PublishAmerica
Baltimore

© 2006 by Ron Pruitt.
All rights reserved. No part of this book may be reproduced, stored in a retrieval system or transmitted in any form or by any means without the prior written permission of the publishers, except by a reviewer who may quote brief passages in a review to be printed in a newspaper, magazine or journal.

First printing

All characters appearing in this work are fictitious. Any resemblance to real persons, living or dead, is purely coincidental.

At the specific preference of the author, PublishAmerica allowed this work to remain exactly as the author intended, verbatim, without editorial input.

ISBN: 1-4241-5586-X
PUBLISHED BY PUBLISHAMERICA, LLLP
www.publishamerica.com
Baltimore

Printed in the United States of America

For Ann,
who believed in me,
even when I didn't.

Heartfelt thanks to the members of the Northwest Arkansas Writers Workshop for their generous support and insightful advice.

Prologue

When he pulled into the drive there was a dead crow lying in the front yard and a flock of crows was making passes, squawking in raucous anger. He parked his old rig and walked over to the bird, trying to understand what had happened. His best guess was that it had flown into the electrical line which passed overhead nearby or had perhaps alighted there and been electrocuted. But he was just guessing. The rain had stopped and the crow lay very still, small on the brown grass. The flock was upset, warning him with wild screeching to leave the downed crow alone. Some of the brasher birds dived at his hat, passing just out of reach and he lowered his head, partly in protection but mostly in solemnity.

He got the sharpshooter and picked up the crow and buried it where it fell. The crows objected, of course. He felt they somehow blamed him for the crow's death and after the crow was buried, they flew back and forth over the grave crying out in protest for most of an hour before they left. They were back the next day, railing at whatever had killed their companion and they kept flying over the place for weeks, still screaming out their charges. It did not matter whether he was outside or not, they made their flyby and screamed murder. He felt guilty by accusation, though he had done nothing except perform a simple dignified burial. In the minds of the birds though, he was guilty by association, and they were determined that the wide world know his crime.

Part I

The Empty Nest

It was still cold when he stepped out on the porch to see what the day was like. He looked out across the fields glistening with frost and nosed into the steam rising from the coffee and took small sips of the scalding brew. The wind was fresh out of the north, the sky so blue it hurt, brushed with high cirrus. The sun squatted low on the horizon, just breaking through the icy mist enough he could feel it begin to warm the denim of his jean jacket. At the far edge of the fields he could see the hawk perched high in its usual old snag, perhaps looking back at him. After a while he tossed his dregs into the yard and went back in the house.

An hour later he was driving through town, blue smoke in the truck's wake. He passed the bank, not open yet, and drove on past gutted storefronts and Redwine's General Store. A few trucks were parked in front of the café and he pulled in beside them and walked in. Some of the men nodded to him, then resumed talking.

He walked over to an empty booth and sat down. He could barely get scooted in and settled before the waitress plunked down a heavy mug of coffee in front of him. A grease slick coated the surface of the coffee and when he picked it up he could see little rainbows reflecting in it.

"Mornin'."

"Mornin, Lonnie, what'll it be today?"

Her name was Ramona, a Choctaw gal, short and stocky, with a broad honest face and greasy blue-black hair plaited in a French braid and make-up so thick it gave her a garish look under the fluorescent lights.

He looked over the menu even though he knew it by heart and then ordered the big breakfast. She jotted it down and ripped it off the pad as she scurried toward the kitchen. He listened to the talk from other tables about livestock, the weather, but mostly about the upcoming Friday night football game with Stigler along with reminiscing about old games, some of them twenty or thirty years back. Most all the men in the cafe, including Lonnie, had been on the team at one time or another.

She came with his order, steaming off the grill on thick ivory crockery webbed with cracks in the glaze. A plate for the eggs, bacon and fried taters. Another loaded with two biscuits the size of his hand and a small bowl of cream gravy lumpy with sausage and specked with black pepper. A big dollop of strawberry preserves. A hunk of butter on a saucer. He gripped the knife and fork and went to the trencherwork.

"I'll be right back with that coffeepot."

When she came back, she stood by the table and visited with him.

"Cold enough for ya?"

"Ain't that bad. Believe it'll turn off nice."

She pushed some dark strands behind her ear. "I been running my legs off all morning. Everybody's all worked up over this game tomorrow night."

He forked up scrambled eggs while she continued talking.

"You'd think these old men was playin' the way they's packing it away."

"In their minds, they is playin' ever much as when they was playin'."

"Well, it's about to wear me out."

"You better not work too hard, the weekend's almost here."

"It's not like I have a choice. I feel like I feed half the men in this town. They just keep showin' up day after day. Don't they have wives at home to feed 'em?"

"Well, you wouldn't want us to starve to death would ya?"

She just gave him a wry look. They bandied about a few more remarks and she topped off the coffee a second time and he asked her if she wanted to go with him to the VFW dance Saturday night.

"I already got a date for that night, but if you come on by, I'll try to save you a dance."

He nodded noncommittally and spooned preserves onto a biscuit.

"You goin' to the big game?" she asked.

"Doubtful."

Before he left town, he stopped by Redwine's to pick up a few things. A slab of bacon, a loaf of light bread, a few onions, a half moon of longhorn cheese, some thick-sliced baloney, a box of crackers, some cans of tunafish and a can of elberta peaches. Mr. Redwine gathered the items as he called them out and set them on the counter in front of Lonnie and then licked the lead of a Laddie pencil, toted it up on a brown bag and sacked them up in the same poke.

"Cash or charge?"

"Charge."

Redwine nodded and pulled out his account book and made an entry.

"Thank ya kindly. You all come on back, you hear," he mouthed ineffectually as Lonnie hit the door. He drove out of town the opposite way from which he had driven in and rolled a few miles down the highway and then he turned onto a dirt road and slowed, dodging potholes for a few miles and listening to the clink of gravel thrown up against the underside of the truck.

He pulled up in the yard of a weathered old farmhouse that stood on a low rise. There was a hand-dug well in the front yard with a short stone wall encircling it. Otherwise, the yard was bare, giving the house a stark lonesome look. Some old hounds lay in the sun on the south side of the house out of the wind. They raised their heads and looked at him but didn't bother to get up.

He stood on the porch and knocked. In the gray rough-hewn slabs that sheathed the house he could see the arcing marks left by the sawmill in the rough boards. He doubted the house had ever been graced with a coat of paint.

The door was pulled open by a worn-looking woman, thin, narrow-faced, her apron stained with grease spots and her forearms white with flour. He touched the brim of his hat.

"Mornin', Lenora."

"Ed's done gone to town."

"I just come from town."

"Well, I don't know. I reckon he coulda stopped off somewheres on the way."

"Well then, would you tell him I come by?"

"I'll tell him."

She closed the door before he could even turn around and step away.

He drove back to the highway and back through town. The bank was open and he stopped and drew out a little money and then headed over to the feed store and bought fifty pounds of cracked corn for the chickens and he set it in the back of the truck by the groceries and then he climbed in the truck and headed out.

At the edge of town, just as the buildings thinned out, a small bent old man was standing with his thumb out and Lonnie pulled the truck over on the shoulder. The old man lifted a gunny sack off the ground and laboredly climbed into the cab and eased his burden down in the floorboard between his feet.

"Much obliged, much obliged," the old man croaked out, wiping his eyes with the back of his hand.

"Old north wind is cold, ain't it? Ya been standin' out there long?"

"Longer than I cared to."

"Where ya headed?"

"Just down the road a ways to Shady Point."

"I'm goin' a few miles in that direction. Glad to have some company."

The old man didn't say anything and when the silence became awkward Lonnie glanced over, and he was staring grim-faced straight ahead through the windshield. The wind had picked up some, and they weaved and rocked down the road under its influence. The old man snuffled and wheezed.

"Let me turn that heater up. This is a drafty old thang."

"Much obliged." More silence, the wind buffeting past in a whistling rush. It was another mile or so before the old man cleared his throat and spoke.

"I lost my woman this spring. She surely was a good 'un,"

"I'm real sorry to hear that."

"Thirty-seven years we was together and she never complaint bout nothin'. She surely was a good 'un. The good lord giveth and the good lord taketh away. That's all the danged old preacher kept sayin'. Don't mean nothin' to me his sayin' that. It don't make me no never mind."

The old man warmed up and commenced talking nonstop. Lonnie drove on past his turnoff while the old man rambled on telling his stories of tribulation. One son drowned in a pond, another shot dead in a hunting accident. The other children moved off to Tulsa or Oklahoma City to earn a living. Three years of bad droughts killed off a substantial portion of his livestock. His daughter had given birth to an idiot child. Most of his sons were drunks. One was in the pen down in McAlester.

He had to interrupt the old man when they reached Shady Point to find out where he lived and then the old man picked up his narrative again while he drove out a dirt road a mile or so to a shacky little house situated among soft maples that had been brutally pollarded back and looked like they had arms amputated at the elbows thrown up to heaven in protest.

"Have to fend for myself now. Have to tend to everthin'," he whined, and then he reached down in the gunny sack and pulled out a couple of cans of potted meat and tried to get Lonnie to take them but he just waved them back into the sack.

"Much obliged then," said the old man reaching for the door handle and grunting as he climbed down to the ground. While Lonnie backed down the drive, the old man shuffled slowly toward the house, bent over and staring at the ground. The old man's sadnesses occupied him as he drove toward home, and though he kept telling himself to drop it, he could not. It felt like a harbinger of where he might be headed.

Just before he got back to the highway, a huge flock of blackbirds flew up from a farmer's field, chattering, moving separately, yet as one, the group so large it moved over the road like a small cloud, winging in ordered formation. Out on the highway, he got stuck behind a school bus making pick-ups and he saw in the faces of many of the children traces of the parents that had been his classmates. He thought about going back into town and trying to track down Ed, but decided it would probably just be a wild goose chase.

Lonnie turned for his old house. On the dirt road three miles from home he had a flat and had to pull over and when he checked the spare it also was down and he spat angrily into the road and grabbed his goods out of the truckbed and started walking. A few cars passed him by but none stopped and it took him a good hour to limp back to his place.

When he walked past the For Sale sign and headed up the long drive he noticed Ed's flatbed parked by the house. As he closed the distance he could see Ed sitting on the porch steps smoking a Pall Mall. By the time he was in the yard Ed had ground out the butt on the steps and flicked it under the porch and then pulled out the pack and shook out a new one and coaxed it out with his lips. When Ed looked up a grin cracked his leathery face.

"Ya taken to walkin' for yer health?"

"Old tar give out on me back down the road."

"Ya could use some new rubber on that old crate."

"I could use a lot of thangs."

He set his bag on the porch and sat down on the steps a little stiffly and stretched one leg out in front of him. Ed took a long drag and exhaled and watched the smoke whisk off in the chill breeze.

"How's the leg?"

"Not too bad."

"Where ya been?"

"Runnin' all over. Went by your place. Lenora said you were out and about. Thought you might have somethin'."

"Well, here's somethin' to level your nerves and ease your

mind." Ed reached down by the steps and brought up a quart fruit jar hall full of clear liquid and held it up high to the light and swirled it around.

"Lordy, give me a sup of that."

Ed handed it across and he unscrewed the lid and took a tentative sip.

"Purty damn smooth. New batch?" He took a second larger swig and handed it back.

Ed grinned his gap-toothed crooked smile, relaxed from the head start he had on Lonnie.

"You wanted some?"

"Shore 'nuf."

"All right." Ed walked out to his truck and rummaged among some firewood ricked up against the cab at the front of the bed and he brought back a full jar and handed it to him.

"You got anothern?"

"Shore do."

He went back to his truck and moved the wood around again and extricated a Ball jar and came back as Lonnie headed up on the porch.

"Let's get in out of this wind. It's cuttin right through me."

"I'm right behind you."

They went in the house and Lonnie set the groceries down and they sat down at the kitchen table and passed Ed's fruit jar back and forth.

"You goin' to the game?"

"Maybe, maybe not."

"Your nephew'll be playin'."

"I know it."

"Hell, he's the best receiver they got."

"Well, I guess he takes after his old uncle that way."

Ed tried to grin at that, but he was in midsup and some of the liquor trickled down his chin and dribbled onto the table.

"You was always a hell of a runner," he said, wiping his face on his sleeve.

"I was tolerable at the time. But I get better ever year that passes now."

"I think you oughta come on down."

"Shit, they'll probly just get their asses whipped by them Stigler boys."

"It don't matter, not to me anyways. You'll just be settin' around here listenin' to the wind blow won't ya? I'll be havin' a good time or tryin' to at least."

"I bet you will."

"It's more'n that. I move a lot of product at them games. If they win folks'll want to celebrate and if they lose they'll want to medicate. Either way I do pretty good."

"You better be careful. They catch you sellin' at the high school games, they'll have your ass in jail for sure."

"I'm always careful. I'm so careful it's borin'."

They drank hard for awhile and began to feel it and fell to talking about the things they would do, if they could, and they finished Ed's jar and Lonnie cracked open a new quart. Ed said, if he could, he'd start bulldozing at the Red River and just keep pushing dirt, especially including Texas, right off into the gulf, and then prop his feet up and watch big old ships sailing by. Lonnie said if he could he'd make Oklahoma its own country and build a tall fence around the whole of it and charge admission at the state line.

"Hellfire, Lonnie, nobody wants to come to Oklahoma. You'd go broke in a week."

"That's where you're wrong. They'd come to lay on the beach and swim in the Gulf."

Their frivolity was interrupted by the jangle of the phone from the front room.

"I meant to tell ya. It was ringin' off the hook when I was settin' out there."

Lonnie stepped away, floor boards creaking underfoot and answered it and talked briefly. The dogs were making a commotion in the yard so Ed couldn't hear the words, but from the tone of Lonnie's voice he could tell the call was more business than social.

"Real estate man," Lonnie said when he came back.

"You got a nibble?"

"Don't know. Says he wants me to come into town tomorrow mornin' and talk about somethin'."

"Could be you got an offer."

"Not likely. If'n it was good news, he coulda give it to me over the phone. If they want you to come down and talk, it's not good."

"Whatta ya think it is?"

"Damned if I know. Guess I'll find out soon enough."

Lonnie walked over to the back door and looked out to see what the dogs were after but they were nowhere in sight. When he turned around he noticed the bagged up groceries still setting there and he started putting them away. Ed lighted up another unfiltered and took a long drag.

"How about that old truck of yourn?"

"How bout it?"

"We might as well go take care of it."

When he walked outside the next morning the wind had died down but there was a low bank of clouds fomenting on the northern horizon looking like a gray blanket that had been haphazardly thrown down on a bed. The sun stood above the treetops and was the color of butter through the dusty haze. He fed the dogs and tossed out some chicken feed and, walking back toward the house, he saw the hawk out wheeling in slow big circles above the bottoms.

When he came out of the house again, he was wearing a clean shirt and was fresh-shaven and his hair was combed and parted to one side and he carried his hat in his hand. He got in the old truck and started it up and let it run for a minute, revving it up to warm the oil. He was running on the spare.

While the tube was being hot patched, Ed and he had lounged in the Dari Barn and ate burgers and fries. Ed had tried to flirt with the plump high school girl who served their food, but she had looked at him like he had dropped down from another planet and went off and hid behind the soft-serve machine until they left.

He got into Spiro just fine and parked outside the café and went in. He sat in a booth by the window and the cook brought him his coffee and he sipped at it until Ramona came to take his order. He ordered a short stack and a side order of ham and she rushed off with his order and he picked up the Tulsa paper and read it halfheartedly until she brought his food and refilled his mug.

Her perfume smelled like roses and he wanted to pass a few words with her but it was Friday and the place was packed full and she was running around like a jackrabbit in a lightning storm so he just smiled and nodded and she gave him a grateful look. He ate his food slowly and deliberately, taking his time and eavesdropping on mundane conversations drifting over from the tables. Finally, he slipped two dollars under the edge of his saucer and walked out into the street.

He still had an hour before his appointment. He walked down to the Rexall Drug and bought a tin of Bayer aspirin and downed four of them with a glass of water from the soda fountain. He wandered around inside Oklahoma Tire and Supply for a while, eyeing radios, pocketknives, guns, all of which he'd considered a dozen times before.

"Just lookin'," he told the salesman when he approached.

It was still too early when he left the store so he walked back to the truck and got in and turned on the radio and listened to the farm and weather reports for a while. He was tired of fooling around town and he was worried in the way an unknown factor can unnerve you and he was hung over from his bout with Ed. He turned the key and the old truck roared to life. It rumbled the four blocks to the real estate office and he parked right out front and walked in.

Mr. Moore will see you shortly, the receptionist said, and sat him down on a fake leather couch to cool his heels a while longer. After a few minutes he heard a toilet flush and a minute or two later Fred Moore's bulk filled the door.

"Come on back, Lonnie."

Moore was a fat man, not moderately so, but obese, an oval on short squatty legs topped by a head that seemed too small to command such a large mass. He wore a black suit, a white shirt and a bolo tie, and his collar cut into his flesh, leaving a band of red welt like a noose had been around it. When he sat down he had to wedge himself into the big padded office chair.

"Sit down, Lonnie, make yourself comfortable. How's things goin'?"

"Goin' good."

"How's your family?"

"They're good."

"Glad to hear it. Lonnie, let me ask you something, if you was to need to, how quick could you pack up and get off your place?"

Lonnie paused, not quite sure how to field the question. "Pretty quick I guess. I done sold off most of the stock, the furnishings ain't much."

He stopped, not sure what else to say.

"Well, Lonnie, it might come to that sooner than we both expected. I've got an offer on your place and I believe the old boy is serious about it."

"How much?"

"Hold on a minute, Lonnie, just keep in mind this is his initial offer."

"How much?"

"Two."

"Two? That ain't even half."

"Yeah, you're right. Don't take it personally. Just be glad we got an offer and I believe he's prepared to go higher."

"He better be prepared to go a lot higher or he can kiss my ass. Who is it?"

"You're not gonna like it."

"I'm gonna have to find out sometime. Who is it?"

"Henry Looper."

Lonnie's chin sagged, his eyebrows arched, and he looked like he smelled something foul.

"Why would old Henry Looper want my little parcel? Hell, he already owns half of LeFlore County."

Moore shrugged the question off.

"He likes land Lonnie and they're not makin' any more of it. It's all above board and his money is good as the next man's."

"Not to me it ain't."

Lonnie stood up.

"I think we're finished."

"Lonnie, sit back down. At least listen to what I have to say."

Lonnie perched on the edge of the chair and stared hard.

"Lonnie, I knew you was gonna pitch a pure cat fit when you heard this. But Lonnie, this is the only offer we got on the table. Don't take this wrong, but your place is not gonna be that easy to sell. It's ten miles out of town, off the main roads and, don't get offended, but it's not in that great of a shape. The house is old and it needs paintin'. If you was willin' to put some money into it and modernize and spruce it up some, I might be able to interest a young family in it, but such as it is..."

He shook his head back and forth gravely and the wattle under his chin swung back and forth like a clock pendulum. Lonnie looked down at the hat in his lap and picked it up by the crown like he meant to put it on.

"It may not be so fancy, but it's some of the finest bottomland you'll find around these parts. Everbody knows the Poteau bottoms will grow anything you stick in the ground. My daddy and granddaddy both made a good livin' off that twenty acres for more than forty years. Now some rich sumbitch comes along and wants to pick it up for a hunnerd dollars an acre. That's insultin'."

"He'll come up, Lonnie, he'll come up substantially."

"I don't care if he comes all the way up to the askin' price, I'm not sellin' to him and that's all there is to it."

"Lonnie, I know you got your reasons for feelin' that way. But farmland don't bring what it used to because there ain't no farmin' these days. Your pa and grandpa mainly raised cotton but the gins been closed down for ten years or more. Yeah, it's good land, some of the best, but these days people can move into a brand new tract house in town for about the same price you're askin'."

"What about ranchin'? That land grows grass so fast the livestock can't keep it eat down. I hope you're not gonna tell me ranchin' is going out of style."

"No, ranchin' *is* big business. In fact, that's the problem. Your piece aint big enough to garner much interest as a ranch. And honestly there's ranch land out there on the market at a lower price."

"I hope this ain't the sales pitch you're givin' to buyers."

The big man rolled his eyes and leaned forward.

"Lonnie, I'm legally obligated to present you the offer. Look at it this way, supposin' it wasn't Looper, it was somebody you don't know and he come close to your askin' price, would you sell?"

"It ain't that way though is it? And I do know that ornery old sum bitch and I don't trust him as far as I could thow him. Old Henry ain't getting my place."

The fat man swiveled his chair and leaned back and looked at the wall.

"Lonnie, are you sure you really want to sell your place?"

"I'm rarin' to sell, but not to Looper."

"Okay, I understand, I'll let him know you rejected his offer."

"I'll bet that won't come as no big surprise."

Lonnie stood up again and walked for the door.

"Lonnie, I think I know how you feel. But go home and calm down and give it some consideration. I don't want to be discouragin' and I'll keep tryin' but I don't know if we'll get another offer."

"I tell you what, Mr. Moore, I'll consider it about the time they start puttin' locks on garbage cans."

Henry Looper stood bent over in his front yard picking dead birds off the ground. They lay scattered under the flowering pears that flanked the path to the front porch. Looper examined each stiff little corpse with satisfaction before chucking it into a tan grocery sack. Mostly sparrows, juncos, and grackles, with a few redbirds, tufted titmice and chickadees. Even a couple of dead crows, their oily black feathers gleaming.

What you get for crappin' in my yard. Goddamned birds. A nuisance. You been ruinin' my lawn for years with your milky, runny shits. A man can't get from the gate to the front door without ending up with some on his boots.

They gathered late in the day, twittering excitedly, pecking at the poisoned grain he put out. He liked to watch from the window as the toxin took effect, as they lost their grip and fell to the ground like ripe fruit, as they jerked in spasms of the death throes. It pleased him.

His hate for the birds was in response to their stupidity, their filthiness and their incorrigible habit of taking his property for their own use. The woods were filled with places they could roost, yet they chose to infest his trees, besmirch his territory. They had no respect. He had no mercy.

The little men had suggested the idea. The birds were irritating him to distraction and he couldn't concentrate on anything else, and their numbers kept increasing as the trees grew and provided more shelter. At first, he had been skeptical of the plan, arguing with his advisors that no matter how many he killed, more just took their place. But, like always, the little men had turned out to be correct. It did require some effort to gather the dead, but he found it an enjoyable task, and the poison worked so quickly, the birds didn't have time to soil his ground.

He bagged up the last of the bodies and climbed the steps and turned and looked back across the bare yard. Shouldn't of messed with me. See what you get.

That evening Lonnie sat out on the porch as the light faded and the sky tinted to indigo and he watched a storm building on the northern flats. He heard coyotes yipping far out on the prairie and the pulsing song of a Kansas City Southern locomotive as it ripped down the tracks miles away. As blackness filled the diorama he could see in the direction of town a fountain of light thrown up, the glow from the football field. To the left of town, blue crackles of lightning trickled along the division between dark sky and darker earth.

It was calm and a chill crept in after sundown and he sat deep in thought going back over the conversation with Moore. Things he wished he'd said. Different wordings to the things he had said. Things he wished he had not said. He went back again to Moore's words, trying to divine the man's true intent and loyalties. And though he kept telling himself to stop thinking about it, the thoughts homed in like steel to lodestone.

Sensing the coming thunderstorm, the dogs joined him on the porch, and he welcomed their company, and began to talk to them about things hidden deep inside him. They listened, heads cocked attentively, and when he was finished they appeared to think about what he had said a good long while until finally an old dog began scratching his ear as if to say, "I don't believe I can help you with that." He had made himself wait until twilight before he uncapped a new jar and before long the liquor numbed him against the cold and he could feel the tension draining out of him through the soles of his boots. For the first time that day he managed a wan smile at some of the remarks he had made in the real estate office.

As he floated free of the day, he became fascinated with the magnificence of the incoming nimbi, their towers illuminated in flash-bulb strobings of pale blue spider veins. In the flickering he could see the thunderheads roil up the benighted landscape, the outflow boundary engulfing and churning up debris. By the time the first reverberation reached the porch, he was enthralled and awed and humbled. The thunder terrified the dogs and they huddled against the house and shivered. Lonnie tipped the jar obliquely draining the last drops and his worries melted into the night and were whisked away on the rising wind. When big cold drops blew in on the ramparts and bolts shot up exploding from the ground and the bones of the old house shook from the aftershock he got up and retired to his bed, pulled the covers up and listened to the downpour clatter against the tin roof. Lulled by the liquor, he lay listening to the assault, the wind howling out a name he could not quite catch and all else lost in the melee.

The next day about noon he set off for the horse races in Sallisaw. He went back and forth on it all morning, first thinking he would go, then deciding not to, and finally changing his mind and going into the bedroom closet he pulled out an old single twelve gauge, broke it open and worked a small roll of bills out of the barrel. Before he left he put on his best jeans and his cleanest dirty shirt and paused in front of the dresser long enough to see a man weathering away, time eroding his strong features leaving trails across his face. He looked away.

The day was warm for November and the sky washed clean and the color of forget-me-nots. The sun whited out a portion of the domed vault and you could not look in that direction bare-eyed. Sunshine flowed down like manna and he rode with the truck window down, the breeze riffling his hair.

On the way he got hungry. He pulled into a little barbeque stand on U.S. 59 on the south slopes of Wild Horse Mountain. A big-bellied man in a dirty white apron talked around the butt of an dead cigar taking his order. He walked over and bought a bottle of pop out of a vending machine while he waited for the food. The sandwich was huge, big as a saucer, slivered pork stacked thick as his hand and hanging off the sides. He sat at a picnic table in the gravel parking lot and ate. You could taste the hickory smoke in the meat, and the sweetness of the pig meat blended with the molasses in the sauce, which was hot with red pepper and made his whole mouth burn. It came with a side order of beans with more meat in them and a milder sauce. He ate quickly and the food was very satisfying and he left a dollar on the table under the pop bottle.

When he got there, the races had already started and as he walked in from the parking lot he heard the trumpeter sound the post parade for what he figured must be the third race. He noted again the fineness of the day and he was glad he had decided to come.

As soon as he got past the gate he bought a program and flipped back to the third race. It was ten minutes until post time. He glanced quickly through the horses in the program, evaluating information on speed, class, recent races. He walked out to the concourse and looked at the tote board. The crowd had two favorites, one going off at three to one and the other even money. The rest were all at ten to one or longer. He went through the program and eliminated four of the horses and looked again through the records of the others. He looked out on the track where the horses were warming up and he found the nine horse and it was a little chestnut gelding with a long neck. When it was five minutes until post time, he walked over and put ten dollars on the nine to place.

When he got back out outside, he ran into his cousin. Homer was a distant relation, many branches away on the family tree. They shared a common great-grandfather and after that the blood thinned out. Homer was about Lonnie's height and build and two years older. In spite of the divergent genealogy, they could have been taken for brothers. Both stood almost six feet and were lean and lanky except for small beer bellies not so big they hung over their belts. Both had dark straight hair and wide deepset brown eyes and coppery faces testifying to some Cherokee blood in the mix.

"Lonnie, you old so-and-so what brangs you out?"

"Same thang as usual I guess."

"Good to see ya. What did ya think of that dadgummed game last night?"

"I stayed home. What happened?"

"They got beat fourteen-thirteen."

"Close one. How'd it happen?"

"They missed an extry point. When that storm came in the playin' conditions got plum awful. Late in the game our boys took it on in and it looked like they was gonna tie it up, but they had to kick the extry point into the teeth of that storm and the kicker slipped and the ball went almost straight up in the air and the wind caught it and blew it back over his head and it landed about the twenty-five and that old wind caught it and it went bouncin' down the field like it was goin' down the side of a mountain. Both teams took off after it but it was movin' pretty good and takin' some crazy bounces and the first player to catch up with it managed to slap it down but then the wind caught it broadside and it started rollin' it down the field like an egg across a tabletop. Boys was tryin' to dive on it but the field was a mudhole and it kept slippin' through their arms like a greased pig and rollin' on down the field. It begin to look like it was gonna roll clean through the south end zone and on out into the dark but a Spiro boy managed to jump on it at their ten and he landed on it squarely and that shoved it down in the mud and it stuck. It was one of the wildest things I've ever seen. It cost them the tie."

"At least they was in it."

"Yeah they was. I believe coach screwed up. Home field you go for two."

The numbers on the tote board were changing, light bulbs rearranging. They both regarded the odds and betting pools. The horses were approaching the starting gate.

"You got this one figured out?" Homer asked.

"I'm down on the nine."

"The nine?"

Homer cackled.

"You get into some loco weed or somethin'?"

"I bet him to place."

"To place? Lonnie, that horse won't be able to *see* second place from where he finishes. And don't you know better than to bet a long shot to place. You always bet a long shot to win."

"Horse don't seem so bad to me."

"Don't seem so bad? Let me tell you about that horse. I think he did somethin' about five years ago. But since then he's never even been close and the only reason they run him anymore is to get in the way. It says in the program he's a nine-year-old, but I know for sure he's at least twelve. I seen his teeth. What makes you think he's gonna suddenly do something special today?"

"Come in third in his last race. Looks like he's comin' into form."

"Hell he did. Where you findin' this?"

"Right here in the program."

He held out the program to Homer fingering the citation.

Homer looked it for a few seconds, and then busted out laughing. He bent over and slapped his knee and howled and when he stood back up he had to wipe away tears.

"Lonnie, this is the second race. We was delayed. A jockey got throwed into the rail in the first race and it took 'em twenty minutes before they got him in the ambulance."

"Oh shit."

Lonnie flipped back to the second race. He looked at the information on the nine horse and it showed no promise. He looked up at the tote board. It was two minutes until post. He looked sheepishly at Homer.

"How do ya see this race?"

"Thought you'd never ask. The one horse is a dog. The crowd

likes the two and they've made it their second favorite. It looks good, comin' down in class, but I just happen to know that it's runnin' hurt. Don't expect it to do much. The big gray gelding comin' out of three has the best chance. Crowd bet him way down. Four horse has a chance. Five horse can't do it. Little black mare in six. Worth a look. All the horses on the outside is long shots. That's the way I see it."

"Who are you on?"

"The four. He's a four-year-old roan gelding, got some blood, been close a couple of times. Lookin' like he might go off about twelve to one."

"How about the mare?"

"She's shown some speed, but she's streaky. You never can tell with them bitches."

"Thanks a lot bud."

The clock showed one minute till post. Lonnie walked rapidly toward the betting windows and stood behind an old Cherokee man playing combinations of exactas and trifectas. When he got up to the window, he put ten dollars on the four to win.

When he got back to the concourse, they were having trouble loading the seven horse. Every time they approached the gate, the horse would balk. They led it in circles and then tried to get it into the gate but it refused. Finally, they blindfolded the animal and two starters locked arms behind his rump and shoved him into the gate and locked him in. There was a long moment of anticipation and then the bell rang.

The two horse came out stumbling to the right and bounced off the big gray breaking from three, the crowd favorite. By the time the two horses recovered the other horses had surged past and the two and three were at the back. The four horse broke well and got the rail and the little black mare ran hard out of six and tucked right in behind the roan. Behind her, the pack formed, with the three eating dirt at the back and the two running dead last.

It stayed that way out of the clubhouse turn and into the backstretch and then the three swung out to get around the four-wide pack and made his move. Running powerfully, the big gray thundered into a furious gallop and moved past the pack, closed on the mare and moved up on the neck of the four and that was the way it was as they hit the final furlong. Around the turn they came, the four saving ground on the inside, dueling with the big gray, the black mare hanging in right behind.

As they hit the top of the stretch, the gray began to fade and fall back like a windup horse running down. The enormous effort of running from behind and swinging wide around the pack began to tell. He slid back past the roan and then the mare passed him and then Lonnie saw something that made his heart soar. The hopeless nine horse had broken out of the pack and was moving up.

Down the stretch the four took over the race clearing two lengths on the black mare, who appeared to be tiring. But making a real run was old number nine who at mid-stretch moved up beside the mare. Somehow the mare found some reserve of speed and they ran along neck and neck toward the wire. The mare was running with her heart more than her legs and the harder the nine came on, the harder she strained. The jockey was whipping her with every stride while her chestnut challenger was under a hand ride and Lonnie could swear it looked like the jockey was trying to rein the horse in.

Twenty yards from the finish, the mare was desperate. She veered out suddenly, bumping shoulders with the nine, knocking him off his gait and it was all she needed to nose him out for second at the wire. There was an inquiry and after a few minutes the stewards disqualified the mare from second and placed her third.

"You lucky sumbitch," Homer said. "Just proves what they say, better to be lucky than smart."

"I told ya that nine horse wasn't so bad. Just have to be a good judge of horseflesh."

"Get out of here. Go get your money."

The four had been bet down to eleven to one by post time but he had bet it to win and it paid a hundred and ten dollars and change. He only cashed place pay on the nine, which had gone off at thirty-five to one, but there was an overlay in the pools and it helped that the horse that won wasn't the favorite. He walked away with three hundred and fifty dollars in his pocket.

Money won is sweeter than money earned, and carries with it a festive air and Lonnie felt it. It made the day. He knew right away it was the kind of thing you remember years down the line. Maybe ten years later he might be sitting in a bar or around a campfire and Homer would turn to him and say, "Remember that time you made that screwed up bet on the nine horse and that sumbitch came in?"

He hit a five to one in the sixth and other than that he backed losers but none of that mattered. He downed six watered down Oklahoma three-point-two beers and bought six for Homer. After the last race, they drove over to Lessley's Café and Lonnie bought and they had thick sirloins and baked potatoes and big wedges of peach pie.

"The people that owns this café is somehow kin to Pretty Boy Floyd," Homer said.

"That a fact? You reckon he stole the money for 'em to buy it?"

"Could be. Dudn't bother me none. Bankers is a bunch of crooks."

It was getting dark when they walked out of the café, a purple patch of sky marking where the sun had dropped. They parted company in the parking lot shaking hands firmly and the last thing Homer said before he went to his truck was, "You lucky old son of a buck."

Lonnie drove up and down the main drag of Sallisaw for a while until he found a bootlegger and bought two fifths of Jack Daniels. When he got out on the highway he pulled out one of the corks and poured some bourbon into his mouth and just let it trickle down the back of his throat. It had the tart taste of oak and a smoky headiness to it. He took small slugs from the bottle as the truck rolled past Short Mountain and began to drone up the south side of Wild Horse Mountain.

A half hour later he entered Spiro and drove through deserted streets and headed over to the VFW hall and parked among the cars and trucks sprawled across the grounds and rolled down his window so he could hear the muffled music escaping into the evening air. He sat in the cab and drank whiskey and as his eyes began to adjust to the gloom, he saw more and more. A group of men leaned against the building near the door smoking and passing a bottle around. A man and woman in a car close to him were making out passionately. Another couple was standing over by an International pickup and from the way they held themselves and flailed their arms around he was sure they were arguing. He saw Ramona come out on the arm of a young rancher and they got in his truck and drove off. Ed walked out with a woman that wasn't his wife, and they strolled out to Ed's truck and stayed there a minute and then they went back in.

Lonnie felt the glow good drink brings. A fingernail moon was rising above the VFW and a light breeze swept out of the south. He waited. Ed walked out alone and he flashed his headlights and Ed altered his direction and ambled up.

"Where you been hidin' out?"

Lonnie told him about his success at the track and Ed hooted and hollered and danced a little jig. Lonnie offered him the bottle and he took it and looked at the label.

"The good stuff'. He tipped it up and his Adam's apple bobbed and then he nodded appreciatively.

"Where's Lucybell?" Lonnie asked.

"Dancin' with some fool. What are you doin' here? It's not much of an outdoor event."

"Nothin', havin' a little drink"

They passed the bottle back and forth and finished it. Ed leaned into the window, an inquisitive look on his face.

"What you gonna do now?"

"Go home I guess."

"You wanna play some cards? I know where there's a game goin on right now."

"Maybe. What about Lucybell?"

"We'll run her home and then we'll cruise out to the game. Here she comes now."

They drove over to her place in Ed's truck. She was a rotund plain-looking woman in a peach double-knit pants suit. Seeing her reminded Lonnie of what Ed had once said, that she looked like she'd make a good wife for a potato farmer. She wasn't stuck up though and helped them christen the second fifth of bourbon on her way home.

"There's this old boy comes up before the judge and he's accused of bein' drunk for five days. The judge asks him, 'Why did you stay drunk for five days?' and the man says, 'They was the greatest five days of my life.' So the judge asks him, 'Why was they the greatest five days of your life?' and the old boy answers, 'Because I was drunk'."

The man telling the story shuffled and dealt the cards by the light of a kerosene lantern set on a big flat rock in a clearing in the woods along the breaks of the Arkansas River. The night was chill and someone had built a big fire and men would get up now and then and go over and stand by the fire and warm themselves until the next hand was dealt. Most of the men had been farsighted enough to bring a folding chair or a camp stool to sit on but Lonnie and Ed had to scrounge up stumps and drag them up to perch on when they joined in.

Every man there was well on the way to being drunk or was there already. Bottles passed in the circle of card players coming from both directions. Every man there had brought something, Ed's distillings being well represented along with hard stuff supplied by friendly local bootleggers. Sometimes a man would have alcohol arriving from both directions and he would have a bottle of bourbon in one hand and a jar of shine in the other and he'd sample both and keep them going in their respective directions. It was doublefisted guzzling. And like most of their poker games it started out being a card game and ended up being a drinking contest.

Like usual it was hard for anyone to gain an advantage because the men all knew everything about each other. They'd gone to school together, worked together, played on teams together, partied together, grown up together. They'd played poker together regularly since they were teenagers. In many ways they were interchangeable. They all lived out in the country, all except Lonnie were married and all drove pickups and wore Levi's and shirts with snaps. They talked alike, walked alike and stood with the same careless slouch. They all owned livestock of some kind and most of them owned horses. They were independent, cocky, and inbred. They preferred open spaces and they liked being left alone.

Lonnie had a good stake and he took it out and threw it down in front of him and some of the men looked at it greedily. A few cards came his way now and then, not enough to make much difference in his stack of bills. It went that way till around midnight. About then one old boy ran out of money and dropped out and another lay down by the fire and passed out.

All the store-bought was gone by then and things would probably have settled down some if Ed hadn't been there resupplying on demand from his truck. The game went on, hand after hand. As the night wore on, Lonnie drank more liberally until he achieved a kind of weightless state. Though it felt like gravity had disappeared, he also felt like the air had gotten thicker between him and the table, and when he moved his arms the air felt cool and viscous. His hands felt like well oiled tools and he could not feel his legs at all. Cards kept floating down in front of him in slow motion, and he tried to get them to improve themselves and make something strong out of themselves. Often the cards were stubborn and uncooperative or just didn't show enough improvement and then he lost money.

Ed was a cagey player. He folded most hands early, staying in only if he had a high pair or four cards to a straight or flush. He bet it up big when he was holding a strong hand, and he never bluffed if he knew there was a player still in the pot who would stick. He could outdrink most everyone there and he usually came out ahead. Even though the men knew each other by heart, still some usually won and some usually lost. You could win if you got good cards and played the percentages and could hold your liquor. You lost if you got bad cards or made bad bets or if the liquor clouded your judgment.

Lonnie got too drunk and it made him bold. He bet up weak hands on the promise they would mature. He refused to be bluffed out in showdowns. Ed kept giving him dirty looks, but he just grinned back and kept throwing money into the pot from his diminishing bankroll. The cards betrayed him, finally, and he ended up losing it all, and then he watched the game and drank some more for a while until he felt completely numb. Ed was doing all right, most of Lonnie's money now in front of him, and wasn't ready to leave. He walked out to Ed's truck and found an old horse blanket and went over behind a big log and wrapped up in the blanket and lay down and found sweet oblivion.

The next thing Lonnie knew he felt cold and wet and like someone was sticking an ice pick into his kneecap and wiggling it around. A line of spittle had dried on his chin, his mouth parched dry as sandpaper. There was a steady pain behind his eyes. He sat up.

Clouds had come in and a misty rain fell like perfume out of an atomizer. Lonnie slowly stood up and leaned stiffly on one leg. Steam rose from the embers of the fire, bottles lay scattered about, someone's coat hung in a tree, but there were no men and no trucks. Lonnie blinked and looked around in disbelief, feeling like the victim of a practical joke.

He went and got the coat and put it on. A thick sheepherder, it fit like it had been tailored for him. He looked around and found his hat and then he went over and stood by the fire looking puzzled.

"Them sumbitches." After a few minutes he started walking, cursing his friends as he went.

He had to concentrate to keep from limping, and he must have looked a little pathetic because after a while an old couple picked him up. The man and woman were on their way to the Spiro Freewill Baptist. On the road an hour and a half before services began, they stoked up the wood stove and had the church warm by the time the preacher got there. Lonnie slumped in the back seat, and when they saw how dissipated and hungover he looked, they fell silent. Fine with Lonnie, whose head rang with every word. They let him out downtown and he walked over to the VFW and his old truck was the only vehicle left in the lot. He got in and drove wearily home.

When he walked in the front door the phone was ringing. He glared at it, wishing it would stop. At that moment he didn't want to talk to anyone. It continued ringing while he went in the kitchen, took the water bottle out of the icebox and took a long draw. He got a tin of aspirin and poured out several into his hand and washed them down with another mouthful of cold well water. Bent over the sink, he took a handful of cold water and splashed his face. The phone kept ringing.

He went and picked it up. It was Ed.

"Lonnie, it's about time you got home."

"How'd you know I just got home?"

"Because I've been standin' here lettin' it ring for about ten minutes."

"Standin' where?"

"The sheriff's office. I need you to come on down and bail me out."

"How am I gonna do that after you cleaned me out?"

"Can you drive over to the house and get some money from Lenora?"

"Can you imagine what she's gonna think?"

"What won't she think is more like it."

They were driving home from Poteau. Lonnie had picked up the envelope of money from a frosty Lenora and when he got to the truck, he peeked in the envelope and it was a stack of twenties thick as his little finger. It only took five of them to post Ed's bail.

"Can't understand why you're actin' all pissy. You was fortunate not to be in there with me," Ed said.

"I'm not pissy, just tired. Surprised you feel so spry."

"I got free board. Breakfast of oatmeal loaded with weevils."

"What about your truck?"

"Impounded. Can't get it back till tomorrow."

"Did they find any liquor in it?"

"Sure they did, I know they did. They was four or five jars left in there."

"They say anything about it?"

"No and they won't. It'll be gone when I get the truck back tomorrow. That'll be the end of it."

"What about the money?"

"Oh, they got that. Being held for evidence. About now I'd say the sheriff is lookin' at new deer rifles in the Monkey Ward catalog. We'll never get it back, that's for sure. It was a tidy little sum, buy a lot of doughnuts."

They were going forty, stuck behind a cowboy pulling a big utility trailer loaded with bales. Lonnie felt too tired and sore to even try to pass. They rode along in a comfortable silence for a while.

"You didn't even draw a felony charge?"

"Nope, just illegal gambling and public drunk. And public drunk is bull."

"Why, because you wasn't in public or you sayin' you wasn't drunk?"

"Both."

The rest of the day Sunday he lay on the couch and napped. He was awakened once by a phone call from Ed Moore, who delivered what he called a counteroffer, though how anything could counter total flat out refusal was hard for Lonnie to understand.

"Three thousand. He come up a whole thousand."

"Pitiful. Tell him we don't need his kind 'round here."

He was up early and out on the porch looking at horizontal lines of undulating clouds, their undersides like the wrinkled belly of a fat gray beast. It was a gloomy day, dark and subdued, with the smell of rain in the cold air sieving into the ratty old truck as he drove to Ed's. For some reason a few large vees of wild geese had decided to have an early morning flyaround despite the threatening weather. They were up there moving in wide circles. These were local geese, wintering close by along the river, and they never left the area, unlike the flights you would see spring and fall, high up there, flying arrows headed to Canada or Central America.

He sat down to breakfast with Ed in the little lean-to kitchen on the back of the house. Lenora shuffled back and forth between the stove and the table and kept their plates full, eggs, sausage patties, biscuits, redeye gravy, and their cups steaming. Ed pushed five twenty dollar bills across the table and tried to get Lonnie to take them for his trouble, but Lonnie acted like he'd sooner pick up a snake. He looked out a back window, across the fields and he could see white mist in the valley, monochrome grayed-out cows in the meadow, the bare orchard etched along the edge of the ice cloud.

When the impoundment yard opened they were there waiting, and Ed pulled a few more notes out of his envelope and ransomed his flatbed. The firewood was still neatly stacked against the back of the cab.

"What you gonna do?" Ed asked.

"Now?"

"Yeah now."

"Nothin' much I guess."

"You wanna go run around with me for a while?"

"Where to?"

"Around town. I need a few bags of corn and a hundred pounds of sugar."

"I see how you are. What you want is a flunky."

"Now you get it. How about it? I'm lonesome."

"I think I just remembered somethin' I need to do."

Lonnie walked out of the little mom and pop grocery with a bottle of Grapette and a cherry fried pie in a small paper sack. It was midmorning and raining steadily straight down and the windows inside the truck were fogged and he took out his handkerchief and wiped off the inside of the glass before he drove on.

At the old folks home, he walked past a dozen or so wheelchaired seniors in the lobby, all either staring at the floor or looking out at the rain. Disinfectant and body musk, the whole building reeked of their combined odors and as he walked past the room next to his father's, an old woman lay in a hospital bed arching her back and pissing into a bedpan.

His father, along with the other old man in the room, was watching a black-and-white *Gunsmoke*. Engrossed by some situation Matt was in, they didn't look up when he walked in. He unbuckled the leather straps binding his father's arms to the wheelchair and the old man rubbed his forearms alternately but still stared at the screen intently.

Matt was in a gunfight on the street with a tall man who wore a bowler and a pin-striped suit with a bow tie and had a big black mustache. Lonnie figured him for a gunslinger or a gambler. They faced down and went for their pistols. Matt missed and the badman shot him in the shoulder and his Colt dropped to the dirt and Chester had to shotgun the shooter from the alley to keep Matt from getting killed. The old men watched all that happened with troubled looks and occasional groans and moans and only looked a little relieved when Doc diagnosed Matt's wound as superficial and Miss Kitty fussed over him.

A commercial came on and Lonnie pressed the grape pop into his dad's right hand and reached into the sheepherder and pulled out a church key and pried off the crown cap. In the other hand he placed the cherry fried pie. His dad looked at him trying to place him, and then looked from one hand to the other, and took a long pull from the Grapette. The old man ate with gusto, some of the pie crumbs going onto his shirt front and grape pop giving his lips a purple cast.

He was just finishing the food when a nurse looked into the room. A young short-haired blonde, attractive in a cookie-cutter way, and Lonnie thought she must be new because he hadn't seen her before, and she spoke in cheerful chirpy tones.

"Mr. Stewart. It's a good day. I see you have a visitor."

His dad was looking at the screen-printed label on the Grapette like he intended to remember the name for future reference.

"Do you know who this is?"

The old man screwed up his face a little and looked over at the television where a game show had started.

"Luke."

"See, he knows you."

"I'm not Luke."

"Oh. Who's Luke?"

"Luke was his younger brother. Drove a tank. Died in France in forty-four."

She nodded. He tried to look her over without being obvious.

"Dad always said I reminded him of Luke."

"So in a way, he did recognize you."

"In a way, I guess."

One evening, he drove north into the Cookson Hills and pulled in at Tuffy's County Line. It was a ramshackle flatroofed affair, part log, part concrete block set back from the highway on the floor of a small draw. The wind had died at sunset and a glistening cupola of stellar fire burned, framed by the dark hills. Only three other cars waited in the unlit lot as he crunched across to the door in the pooled blue starlight.

When his eyes adjusted to the near darkness in the bar, he could see two young Cherokees sitting quietly in a booth and a pair of cowboys in another, their legs stretched lengthwise along the padded seats, backs against the outside wall. Tuffy stood behind the bar, looking bored. They all looked up when he pushed through the door, but gave him no more than a glance.

Smack down the middle of the plank floor a white line about the width of a stripe on a basketball court had been painted. It was the county line, dividing Cherokee and Sequoyah counties and it was the loophole that made Tuffy his living. The bar owner took advantage of a long standing feud between the sheriffs of the respective counties. Though hard liquor was illegal in the state, Tuffy served it with impunity, but he kept the bottles on a wheeled cart and watched the door closely. If lawmen from Cherokee County came into the place, he wheeled the cart across the line into Sequoyah County, and vice versa. If he got word the federal boys were in the area, he pulled the hard stuff out of the building and outwaited them, serving only pisswater Oklahoma beer until it was safe for him to pour whiskey again. Tuffy had survived and prospered this way for most of two decades and he made generous contributions to the campaigns of both sheriffs to help keep them in office and further the standoff as long as possible.

Lonnie stood at the bar and sipped at a shot of good bourbon.

Tuffy had the potbellied stove fired up and it was toasty and he took the sheepherder off and hung it over the back of a chair. He had three whiskeys and was drinking a beer when Leonard came in and walked over. The big Cherokee eased down fluidly onto a bar stool.

"Kinda operatin' on Indian time ain't ya?"

Leonard just looked at him darkly and pulled out a pouch and began building a smoke. After he fired it up, he signaled Tuffy over and ordered a whiskey and a beer back and sat silently waiting for them to arrive. They sat around drinking for a while, not saying anything, Lonnie waiting until Leonard was ready to talk. Finally, he piped up.

"I seen me a cougar."

"When?"

"T'other night, bottom of Boudinot Hill, crossed the road right in front of me."

"Doubt it was a cougar. Coulda been a big wildcat. Maybe a polecat, a big tom."

"Cougar, fer sure. Old man runs the gas station at the junction says he's seen it moren oncet."

"I never heard tell of such a thing in these parts. Bear I could believe but not a mountain lion."

"I had to brake or I woulda hit it. It was long as me and it turned its head and looked right at me and its eyes glowed big and yellow as a demon's."

"Maybe that's what it was, a demon come out to get ya."

"Naw, it was a cougar. There ain't no demons."

"Ain't no cougars round here neither. How much had you had to drink?"

"I didn't imagine it. I seen it."

"If you say so."

Lonnie bought another round of shots. He inquired after

Leonard's family. They talked about the weather, people they both knew, shared history.

"I'm selllin' out."

"You're not."

"I am if I can find a buyer."

Leonard looked at him funny, like he didn't really know what to say.

"What you gonna do?"

"I don't know. Get the hell outta Dodge."

"I never knowed you wanted to."

"Well, it's a long road that dudn't turn."

"What about your daddy?"

"What about him? He won't know."

"He might."

"No, he won't. He don't know nothin' no more."

"Always thought you had a nice little place. Sheltered. Good water. Close to the river."

"Maybe you oughta buy it."

Leonard looked at him and blinked and things began to fall together in his head.

"Ain't got the money."

"Maybe we could work somethin' out. Could you come up with a thousand or so? I'd carry the rest."

"Maybe, probly not".

"What could you come up with?"

Leonard thought on it a while.

"Might be able to get together a few hunnerd."

Lonnie nodded.

"Think about it some. Can't do nothin' now till I get it out of the hands of the real estate man."

"You listed your place?"

"'Fraid I did."

"It sure is a pretty place. Ain't you gonna miss it?"
"Yeah, I will some."
"But you're goin' ahead on anyways."
"For certain I am."

His sister caught up with Lonnie on the boardwalk outside Redwine's. She looked like a smaller more finely chiseled version of him, with straight dark hair long enough to hang down her back but put up neatly in a bun.

"I'm mad at you."

"How come?"

"Because you ain't been over for so long and I didn't even see you at Little Lonnie's game."

"I intended to come, but then that storm blew in. How'd he do?"

"He caught ever ball they thowed to him, even in the pourin' rain."

"He's a player, maybe he can even go to the Sooners. That'd be somethin'."

"Could be, if he don't get hurt, or flunk out or get some girl pregnant and ruin his life. I'll tell you this, that game must take a lot out of a person cause your nephew can eat more than any human I ever seen. I keep fillin' up the icebox with all kindsa food, and he keeps emptyin' it out."

"Yeah, dad used to eat like that. Mom would make those huge meals all the time and dad would eat all evenin' until he fell asleep in his chair. Little Lonnie's always reminded me of his grandpa. Ya been over to see Dad lately?"

"I went over last Sunday after church and took him some dinner. He was asleep or they had him knocked out on drugs because he was really out cold. I left the food with the nurses. I sure hope they gave it to him when he woke up."

"I was over there. He was awake, seemed all right, good appetite. We looked at a western together on the television set. He's about the same, I'd say."

She nodded and he noticed worry wrinkles by her eyes and blue shadows underneath.

"I'm gonna keep on prayin'."

She invited him to Sunday dinner and told him if he didn't come around more often his nephew was not going to recognize him on the street.

"Maybe I'll come on over then."

"You better. I'm making fried chicken."

It was a two-hour drive to Tulsa but it was a fine late fall day, polar blue sky flecked with scraps of high clouds, true morning light, no wind. The old truck parsed the highway, wind whistling tunes through the air seeps, the beat of the tar strips in the concrete joints keeping time.

Sallisaw, Vian, Webbers Falls, following the big river north and east to Muskogee and Slick's Barbeque. About noon Lonnie was sitting on a wooden bench in the packed ribhouse waiting for his order. It came quickly, served by a dusky beauty with a sassy walk. A pile of ribs, still smoking from the grate, on top of two pieces of light bread and a thick slice of raw onion. Sauce on the side, sweet, pungent, a rich hint of honey lingering after. The meat was tender and falling off the bones and as quickly as they cooled, he coated each rib with sauce and ate it savoring each and every bite.

Early afternoon, he crossed the Arkansas River for the third time at Bixby and soon traffic began to thicken and the scattered hamlets on the outskirts of town came into view. He was a little early, so he stopped at a J.C. Penney and shopped for a while and before he drove over to the school he gassed up the truck.

He was parked out front when the bell rang and the students came pouring forth, happy with their daily dose of freedom. He watched them stroll out and walk for the street and they kept rolling out like water going downhill. Then he saw Clay step out alone wearing wheat jeans, a striped oxford cloth shirt and pointy boots. The boy walked swiftly with long strides and he watched him walk and it reminded him of a good colt he'd once owned. He got out and went and intercepted him.

"You have practice?"

"No, I didn't make the team."

"How come?"

"Mostly because I'm too short and too slow."

"Thought you could at least play some guard."

"No, my ball handling ain't that good."

"Well damn."

"It ain't that easy here. Instead of a hundred guys in the whole school, there are seven hundred. And at least fifteen of them have a better game than I do."

"There's always baseball and track in the spring."

"Yeah there's that."

They sat in the truck in front of the Dairy Queen eating huge vanilla cones.

"They don't let you wear these here."

"Jeans?"

"Blue jeans."

"In Tulsa?"

"No, to school."

He had given him the clothes he had bought for him. Button-up Levi's and a black and white checked western shirt with pearl snaps.

"But wheat jeans they're allowed?"

"Yeah. Thanks, it'll be fine."

"So it's the color that's the problem."

"It ain't a small town school. I can wear the shirt up there to school just fine."

"You can wear the Levi's on the weekend."

"Sure. I can use 'em. I have a whole bunch of new clothes Mama went out and bought, but it's all this stuff that makes me look like I'm goin' to church. She's got ideas about the way city folks dress."

"You know what I think? Anyone who dudn't wear Levi's is suspect. Lawyers, preachers, real estate folk, insurance men, you have to watch them close as you would a poisonous snake. Course some of the ones that wear Levi's is snakes too."

Lonnie began crunching into his cone and finished it quickly. He started the truck and drove over and parked in front of a red brick bungalow in a newer neighborhood.

"How's your mama?"

"She's all right."

"Is she goin' to have a tizzy about me comin' by?"

"Not if I don't say anything. She dudn't get off till five."

Lonnie nodded thoughtfully.

"How are things with old Larry?"

"Old Larry don't say much to me. He's not around most of the time, comes home late, sometimes I don't see him for days. I know he talks to mama. It's strange because he barely says a word to me, but mama says he wants to adopt me."

"Adopt ya?"

"Yeah, they're talkin' about goin' to see a lawyer."

"What do you think about all that?"

"Bunch of bull if you ask me. I'm not changin' my name to Looper."

"You're durn tootin'. I'd a lot rather be a Stewart than a Looper. Hellfire, boy, we're descended from the kings of

England. Besides I always thought Looper was a kinda goofy name. Anyway, you're the only one left to carry the Stewart name forward."

"Yeah, that's just what I think. It's probly just talk. They talk about all kinda crazy stuff."

"Let me know if it gets past the talk stage. Not that I want to cause trouble but I would over that. Anyway what's it like to live in the big town?"

"It ain't all that bad. Ever Saturday I got a choice of about a dozen picture shows. There must be ten or fifteen radio stations. I can take auto mechanics next year when I'm a senior. People won't hardly give you the time of day, though."

"What else does your mama say? What do they talk about?"

"She says next year soon's I'm old enough Larry wants to buy me a car. He never said nothin' to me about it. I don't want it anyway. Rather have a horse."

There was a backboard in the drive and before he left they went one-on-one for half an hour and it was a close game, the son quicker, more agile, the father stronger, more experienced. In the cool fall air the ball hung fat and orange and when the eye and hand were together the ball floated like a planet in orbit and passed through the ring without touching it and continued its parabolic flight until it collided with terra firma and the shooter took it back behind the line. When it was tied twenty baskets each, Lonnie proposed sudden death and Clay drove the lane, faked right, pulled up and hit a jumper.

"Lucky shot."

"That was skill."

They sat in the drive cooling down and catching their breath until the bells of a distant church rang out five o'clock and he got up and said his good-byes and drove away.

Henry Looper sat up ramrod straight across the desk from Sheriff Johnson. He reached into the vest pocket of his suit coat and took out a legal envelope and slid it across the desk. The sheriff peeked inside and then stuck it in a drawer.

"Can you do it soon?"

"First chance I get."

"You got a man you can trust?"

"Believe I do. He's done this kind of thing a few times. Never let me down oncet. Remember a coupla years back, that old boy ran into my sister's car? Made a big fuss. Claimed it was all her fault. Some slick lawyer got him off."

"I heard he left town."

"He's still around, but he won't be causin' nobody no grief. You might say he's gone underground."

The sheriff gave Looper a knowing look and the old man grinned crookedly, like he was relishing an inside joke.

"I need you to keep your mouth shut about all this. It's a family matter. Like it settled quiet. Kind of like your deal."

"The three of us is all that'll know anything. I'll caution my man to be sure to keep it to hisself. Won't breathe a word to nobody. Another thing I like about him, he's tight-lipped."

"It better not get out. It does, I'll come back in here and make you wish it hadn't. I don't put up with sloppy work. In my time, I've seen sheriffs come and I've seen sheriffs go. You wanna hang around here a while, you'll make sure this is did right."

The sheriff suppressed a smile at the frail old man's threat and tried to look serious, knowing it was just part of the old timer's blustery routine. Old Looper looked shrunken, the suit he wore too big for him, and there was a gap between his skinny neck and the stiff starched collar of his shirt. On the other hand, Looper did carry a lot of local weight, a lifetime of building friends in powerful places.

"You got nothin' to worry about. I'm gonna make your problem disappear. People forget fast. A month from now, it'll be old news."

"Tell your boy to be careful. This ain't no dumb clodhopper. He's right savvy and could give ya trouble. Hard-headed little prick. Got no respect for nothin' or nobody."

"I think my man can handle it. He's meaner than a nest of rattlesnakes and enjoys his work."

Looper nodded, satisfied. He stood, and turned for the closed door. His hand on the knob, he looked back over his shoulder.

"Don't half-ass it. That'd be the worst thing you could do."

"I'll keep that in mind."

The sheriff watched Looper shuffle away and then picked up his phone and dialed a number from memory.

Part II

Ruffled Feathers

Leonard looked uncomfortable. His big frame was hunched on a metal chair in the loan department at the Cherokee County State Bank. A middle-aged man with metal-frame glasses sat with a pen poised over a loan application, making a list of Leonard's limited assets.

"So you want to put up two cows and eight horses as collateral for a secured loan of a thousand dollars?"

The big Cherokee nodded.

"And you work seasonally in your own landscaping business?"

The bank manager looked up at him. Leonard looked back. The banker tapped the pen on the desktop.

"Do you have any other source of income? Does your wife work?"

"Sure she does. Ever day."

"Where does she work?"

"Around the house."

The banker marked through something he had written on the form.

"I see your home mortgage is with us. You've been late with a few payments."

"We're caught up now, late fees and all."

Leonard noticed frown lines etched at the corners of the banker's mouth.

"Do you receive any tribal benefits?"

"Indian hospital."

"Any stocks, bonds, royalties?"

"Not hardly."

"May I ask why you need the money?"

"Down payment."

"What type of property are you seeking to acquire?"

"Farm."

"Do you have financing approved for the real estate transaction?"

"Owner's an old friend. He'll carry me."

"So you would be making payments to him while simultaneously paying off the loan you are seeking?"

"Something like that."

The banker curled his upper lip and tapped the pen against his front teeth.

"Tell me about these horses and cows."

"Couple of skinny yearlings and a bunch of old horses."

"The horses, are they breeding stock, rodeo horses, cattle horses. Anything like that?"

"We use em for riding trails."

"Recreational purposes." The banker made a note and then turned the paper toward Leonard.

"Sign right here to authorize us to check your credit. I

should have an answer for you one way or the other by next week."

Leonard carefully signed at the bottom of the page.

"What do you think it'll be?"

"I'd hate to speculate."

"Go ahead. Take a guess. I won't hold you to nothin'."

"Well, sir, your financial profile is not that strong. And the late payments don't help. The loan committee doesn't like taking risks. But let's wait for a final decision from them and hope for the best."

Leonard stood up, towering over the desk. The banker rose and stuck out his hand and Leonard just looked at it.

"Seems like the only way you can get a loan here is if you don't need it."

A large shadow fell over Lonnie's plate and he looked up from his chicken fried steak to see Ed Moore looming over him, a forced smile on his face. A patch of cream gravy spotted his black vest.

"I've brought you an attractive offer. I think you should take it."

Lonnie put down his fork and wiped his mouth.

"Tell me all about it."

"Four thousand and the buyer pays all closing costs."

"Anybody I know?"

"For the purposes of this transaction, the buyer wishes to remain anonymous. The property will be transferred into my name as a silent partner."

"Old Uncle Henry again?"

"I'm not at liberty to discuss the identity of the buyer. But it's a good offer. I doubt we'll get a better one."

"The money's close. But you're still tryin' to get me to sell to the one person on the face of the earth I won't have anything to do with."

"I'm just trying to make my commission and help you find a buyer. I think I've done that."

"You haven't shown the place to a single soul. If you were really tryin', we might have a buyer by now. I'm beginnin' to wonder who you represent, me or Henry Looper. No, that's not exactly right. I'm startin' to understand that all you want to do is push this deal on me. Let me ask you somthin'. Has old Henry offered you something extra if you can swing this?"

Moore looked uncomfortable and his face glistened with sweat. He leaned forward and put his fingertips on the formica tabletop.

"Now you listen, Lonnie, and you listen good. You can walk away with money in your pocket, or you can leave this town with the clothes on your back. Or maybe you won't even leave at all. Maybe one day you'll just up and disappear. It's happened before."

Lonnie edged out of the booth and stood up.

"You threatenin' me? I'll drag you out in the street and whip your ass."

"I'm givin' you some good advice you're too pig-headed to take."

"How bout this. I'll give you two hunnerd to tear up our contract. Money for doing nothin'. Can you beat that?"

"How about if you just live up to what you promised to do?"

"I never had any notion to sell my family plot to that crazy old reprobate. My mama would roll over in her grave."

The old cook approached them and gave them a steely look. Lonnie noticed some of the lunch crowd darting glances in their direction.

"Boys, you need to take this outside."

Lonnie marched out and Moore trudged after him and caught

him before he got to his truck. On the sidewalk, they faced each other down like gunfighters.

"Lonnie, you've got to look at this as a business deal and stop letting your personal feelings get in the way."

"How much longer does your contract run?"

"About five months I reckon."

"I'll just wait it out. Don't bother me no more with your tomfoolery."

"You're 'bout the stubbornest man I ever known. People warned me about you. Guess they were right."

"Just know my own mind is all."

Lonnie stuck a toothpick between two front teeth and walked for the truck. Moore stood and watched him back out and chug off, the old truck rattling and laying down a smelly cloud of oily smoke. Moore coughed into his handkerchief, wiped off his face and shook his head in dismay.

The waitress came and cleared the dirty dishes and they ordered dessert and coffee and Ramona chose banana pudding and Lonnie went for a piece of lemon meringue pie. They were in a log steakhouse decorated bunkhouse style with branding irons and old half-trees hanging on the barnwood walls. The savory smell of fried onions and hush puppies drifted from the kitchen. They had heartily downed the entrees, flame-grilled filets, mashed potatoes and gravy, fried okra, corn on the cob, buttered hot rolls. Lonnie felt bloated and logy, but happy. When the desserts arrived they picked at them and ate them slowly and talked sipping their coffee.

"You're a good eater."

"I can eat a lot for a short woman."

She did look good, coppery and pretty, lots of eye make-up, hair washed and raven dark, brown eyes big and wet.

"You can eat a lot for a truck driver."

"Truck drivers can't keep up with me."

They nibbled at the sweets and looked at each other and sipped coffee from real china coffee cups. She wanted to know why he was selling out.

"It's not that you have to, is it?"

"No, it's not that. I can't do much work anymore but I got my Army pension. It's not much but it's enough to get by on. I can live on it. Barely."

"So it ain't too late too change your mind and just stay around?"

He took a long sip and looked across the restaurant at an old couple silently eating.

"No, it probly ain't too late."

"So what's this all about?"

"All what?"

"You and me, why are we here havin' dinner together?"

"I thought you wanted to."

"I did, I do. I mean, why are you tryin' to get somethin' goin' with me if you're just goin' to ride off into the sunset first chance you get."

"First chance? I'll be lucky to get a chance."

"But you want to?"

"Yeah, I do."

"I just don't get it I guess. Did you just wake up some mornin' and say I think I'll sell everything I own and go off and live somewhere I don't know with total strangers. That seems like a good idea."

Lonnie chuckled.

"No, wouldn't like that, more gradual like. Tell me this, what's so wonderful about this place?"

"Nothin', 'cept we know it. We know the ins and outs,

where all the lines are not to cross, who to look out for, who'll help you out. I used to think like you do, big wide world out there. So I went out there when I was younger, and it was like ships in the night, people didn't even look at me, so I came back. There's nothin' really special about this place, but it's where my family lives because they all had the bad luck to be borned here."

"Yeah, I know what you mean. Lordy, my family has been plowin' the same ground for about a hunnerd years now. Most people think that means I should go on livin' on that same piece of dirt. But the way I see it is, maybe we done spent too many years in this backwater. Maybe it's time somebody did somethin' different. I guess I could just go on livin' here until I die. It's what everbody expects me to do. The men in my family have been doin' it forever."

"How about the women?"

"Them too. I don't think mama ever got more than a hunnerd miles from here."

"I guess I understand what you're getting' at. Sometimes I feel like this place is plum wore out for me. But you're ingnorin' the most important part, are you goin to up and run off just about the time things are finally getting' interestin'?"

"Between you and me?"

"You got anything more interestin' goin' on?"

"I'm not running away from *you* and as for interestin', you can never tell about that."

"Who or what are you running from then? I didn't think you had any more or less skeletons in your family closet than most of us do."

"Memories mostly. Actually it's a lot more like everbody else run off from me. You could look at it that away."

"That's probly not a real healthy way to look at it and I'm not sure you can run far enough or fast enough to get away from bad memories."

"Probly not. But at least I won't be reminded of them ever day of my life."

"Are you movin' off to Tulsa? I could understand that."

"I don't think I could live in that town. Or any big town. Don't like bein' fenced in."

They left and drove over to the piano bar at the Holiday Inn out on the highway and they drank illegally served white wine and listened to a blind man play jazzed up old standards on an old upright piano. They danced to some of the slower songs and it felt good to hold her. She oozed warmth and moved smoothly and gracefully in his arms. After a while, she moved in closer and rested her head on his shoulder. He could feel soft flesh under his hand and her hair was thick and lustrous as a horse's mane.

"It sure took a long time to get a second date," she said.

"Only about twenty years. You remember that first one?"

"Sure I do. We went to the truck stop at Sunset Corner and ate big meals and you knocked a big glass of sweet tea in my lap and I got soaked and had to go home and change. I think you might have been a little nervous." She grinned mischievously.

"Is that why you wouldn't go out with me again?"

"I would have gone out with you again. You never asked."

"I guess I was embarrassed about the spill. I thought I'd made a bad impression. And then before long I was involved with someone else."

"Janeen. Senior year."

"Right."

He took her home and walked her to her door. Before she went in she turned back one more time.

"In one way you have to count this night as a big success."

Lonnie looked at her expectantly.
"You didn't spill a single thing."

Sunday afternoon was fresh but sunny, and he drove down by the river and parked the truck in a grove of sycamores and walked down onto the sand all the way to the river and stood watching it roll by brown and glassy. In the shallows on the other side a green heron waded around. He gathered driftwood and built a fire on the beach and kept it going all afternoon while he searched the beach for rocks. The Arkansas washed down rocks for eight hundred miles and deposited them along its course. Red jasper from the Colorado Rockies, gray flint from Kansas, pink chert from the Osage country of northern Oklahoma, olivine washed from railbeds, geodes which cracked open to reveal sparkling hemispheres, sharks' teeth, limestone fossils and the occasional arrowhead or stone tool. They were all there in the sand, buried, until storms or floods uncovered them and they surfaced. He walked the dunes all afternoon, bending over to inspect the river's castings until he was tired out on his feet and he lay down on the sand by the fire and took a nap.

When he woke it was late in the day and the winter light was slanty and gray. He sat up and stretched out his arms and a great blue heron came skimming up the current, pterodactyl-like in the gathering gloom. He threw on more wood and lay by the leaping fire and looked at the treasures he had gathered. The evening light glowed orange and across the river a few Canada geese landed setting off widening concentric rings. It began to get cooler, the sun dimming out toward sunset and the wind went down and the sky was in the river all pink with stretched-out lavender clouds.

He felt a little stiff so he got up and limped around the fire a few times to warm up and then he walked over to the truck, leaving the rocks on the sand because seeing them was enough.

He was about to open the truck door when the heard the threshing in the brush. The sound came from a little grove of sumac and he moved quietly toward it and there on the ground a kestrel was flopping around in the leaf litter. It turned and tried to run when it saw him, but it just fell over and didn't have the strength to get up again. It lay there breathing rapidly, looking angrily up at him in the waning twilight.

He gathered the small hawk up and put it in on the seat beside him in the truck. The bird seemed to have fallen into unconsciousness. When he arrived home, he found a bushel peach basket and put an old towel in the bottom and laid the hawk on its side. Except for almost imperceptible shallow breaths, he would have taken the bird for dead. He put the basket in the quiet darkness of his bedroom closet and closed the door on it.

Ed was late and Lonnie had sat on the bar stool at the Red Star an hour waiting for him and was about ready to give up. He kept drinking the three point two beers the barkeep set in front of him, but after half a dozen he still couldn't feel anything, except a little lighter in the pocketbook. It was past quitting time and the beer joint was filling up with day workers, dump truck drivers, dry wallers, ditch diggers, landscapers, road crews, men who made their living with their hands. Satisfied with themselves for getting in another day, they joked, taunted, and eyed a tired-looking middle-aged barmaid who scurried around gathering up empties.

A vaguely familiar-looking big man with the wide shoulders of a weightlifter or a former football lineman settled onto the stool next to Lonnie. He was dressed a little more nicely than most of the others, a crisp gray uniform shirt stretched tight across his chest. He paid for his longneck from a fat roll of greenbacks, casually laid the stack of bills down in front of him, and glanced around the bar with a challenging gaze. He emptied the bottle in two long chugs, clicked it down on the bar and stared at the barkeep until he brought a fresh one. Then he swung around and leaned back against the bar and spoke, looking straight ahead.

"Somethin' smells real bad in here, like some cowboy didn't bother to scrape the shit off his boots."

Lonnie looked down at his worn Acmes, then across at the hand-tooled boots with metal toes the big man wore.

"Maybe it's just your breath."

The big man looked at him and smirked, sucked down his beer, and watched a pool game in progress between two Cherokees. Lonnie noted a fat diamond ring by a hairy knuckle.

"No, I think it might be some cowman hasn't had a bath for about a month. Real rank, like he might be part skunk." Gray shirt held up his empty and eyed the barkeep.

Lonnie looked at the door. A man who loaded trucks at the feed mill came in.

"There's worse smells. Like chicken shit."

He got up and crossed the floor and went in the dank dusky pisser and began draining off the beers. The door clicked open and a man stood beside him at the metal trough. Lonnie didn't look over. Bathroom etiquette.

He never saw the blow coming that caught him on the cheekbone just below the eye, but he felt the ring tear through his flesh and he fell sideways onto the floor and lay half-conscious on his side in a pool of piss, blood dripping off his face. He drifted in and out of darkness. The concrete floor was cool as the other side of the pillow and he could smell musty dried piss and ammonia. The toe of a boot caught him in the kidney and the pain jolted him awake and he rolled away and tried to climb to his feet. He was halfway up when a fist slammed into his mouth, his lip split with a searing pang and he fell backwards into the wall. Blood filled his mouth. He spat and a tooth ticked on the concrete floor.

He sat up and leaned against the wall, looking at the steel-toed boots. When the right one kicked for his face, he threw himself at it, like grabbing for a fumbled football, and grasped the instep with both hands and put his body into it and twisted it as hard as he could. The big man did a little dance on his left foot trying to keep his balance and struck a glancing blow off the side of Lonnie's head. He hugged the boot against his chest and got his feet under him and pushed up with his thighs bringing the leg up as he rose. Big boy toppled over backwards and the back of his head bounced off the edge of the toilet with a hollow thud and he flopped down on his back. Before he could recover, Lonnie stomped his boot heel into the man's gut and he rolled onto his side and curled into a ball and Lonnie kicked him in the back of the head as hard as he could twice, driving his face into the wall. He heard the man groan and then saw his body slouch into unconsciousness.

He stood there spitting blood and saliva into the toilet. The man moaned low and rolled over on his back. Blood flowed from his nose reddening his mouth and chin and eyes were rolled back. A few more seconds and he would have hit the door. Instead, gray shirt revived, struggled to all fours, and it was not until after he lunged at him that Lonnie saw the dull flash of the knife.

Lonnie dodged back against the wall as the knife slashed at his throat. The blade missed his jugular but cut into his shirt at the top of his chest and he felt it grate against the breast bone as it cut through the thin layer of flesh all the way across. Blood welled up and streamed down his shirtfront. Before the knife slashed back in a return motion, he drew back his fist with a compact piston-like smoothness and slammed it squarely into the end of the big man's nose.

There was a snap as the nose bone broke and Lonnie felt

cartilage squash flat under the blow. Gray shirt squealed and his left hand went to his face, like he was trying to keep his nose from falling off. Lonnie grabbed the knife arm with both hands and bent the wrist down until the blade clattered to the floor. Then he sent a swift uppercut into the solar plexis and the man went down to his knees gasping for air. Lonnie put the sole of his boot on the knife blade and reached down and snapped it in two and left it lying there.

He went to the sink and splashed cold water on his face. He felt woozy, like he might pass out and the room spun like he was on a merry-go-round. He stuck his head under the tap and let the water run over his head. He dried his hair on the dirty roll towel and when he looked down, he was still unzipped. With sore fingers, he closed the metal teeth, then tugged at the top of his jeans, and looked over at the big man who lay in a fetal position holding both hands over his shattered face.

He reeled out the door light-headed. Ed stood by the bar, a Pabst held casually in his hand. He looked at Lonnie's bloody, ravaged face and slit shirt. Heads turned and conversation died when the drinkers saw Lonnie dripping a bloody trail onto the floor.

"What happened to you?"

"Little disagreement with some old boy."

The bartender walked over to the bathroom and looked in. He crossed quickly over to where Lonnie was applying napkins to his gashed chest.

"Mister, I'd say you'd best get out of here right now."

Ed shook his head.

"Can't take you anywhere."

Forty-four stitches to close the slit across his chest, ten to suture the gash on his cheek. The old doctor sewed him up with a curved needle without benefit of anesthetic, wrapped his chest with gauze and told him to come back in a week to get the stitches out. Ed was in a jovial mood, a kind of post-fight euphoria, the way a sports fan will savor a victory he had no part in. On the ride to the doctor, he had demanded a blow-by-blow account. Lonnie had supplied details reluctantly.

"So who was this old boy you beat the crap out of?"

"Didn't catch his name. We weren't properly introduced."

"You recognize him?"

"Not really. May have seen him somewhere. Can't place him."

"What's he look like?"

"Big un. Looked like an athlete. Had on a shirt maybe could be part of a uniform."

"Military?"

"City or county. Could be a cop shirt."

"What kind of knife?"

"Huntin' knife. Six-inch blade."

Ed wrinkled his nose.

"You smell kinda bad."

"That's what he said and you saw what happened to him."

After, in the clinic parking lot, they sat in Ed's truck and took a few nips from a quart of moonshine and Lonnie began to feel the pain ease. They were sitting there when the sheriff's car roared up behind them and squealed to a stop and Johnson got out and pulled his weapon.

"Get out of the truck with your hands where I can see them."

"Oh, shit," Ed said. "Now what's this all about?"

Ed capped the jar and stuck it under the seat and they slowly climbed out and faced Johnson, who held his pistol on Lonnie.

"Put your hands on the truck. Stewart, you're under arrest."

"For what?"

"A and B and disturbin' the peace. Had a call from the Red

Star. You put a man in the hospital. You're goin' to jail. Get your goddamn hands on the truck."

Johnson waved the pistol for emphasis. Lonnie faced the truck and put his palms flat against it.

"This is bullshit," Ed said.

"Shut up or I'll take you in too."

Johnson walked forward quickly and came up behind Lonnie and kicked his feet apart and dragged his legs back with a hard jerk on his belt. Then he put his gun in his left hand and used his right to grab Lonnie's arms, one at a time, and cuff them behind him. He perp-walked Lonnie to the cruiser and opened the door and forced him in, shoving his head down forcefully

The sheriff drove to the lock-up, Ed following along behind, and he went in to post bail, but it took four hours before the paperwork was ready, and it was the early hours of a new day before Lonnie walked out a free man.

Ed was bent over a bank shot to the side pocket and he concentrated squinty-eyed on the target ball and stroked. The ball caromed off the side cushion and headed for home but it grazed the corner of the cushion thinly and oscillated back and forth in front of the pocket and came to rest hanging on the lip. Ed hung his head in disgust and sat down and picked up his beer.

Lonnie chalked up and knocked in the cripple lagging the white ball downtable to set up an easy angle to the corner pocket. He made the shot and followed with a difficult combo that made Ed look like he might vomit. Ed never liked losing at anything. The table opened up and he made three straight angles, none of them very difficult. The eight ball came up and it was a spot shot with a chance of scratching. He hit the cue ball high right and hard and the black ball jumped into the hole like a gopher and the white ball went off three rails and rolled to the center of the table and set there spinning.

Ed racked and walked over to the bar and bought two beers while Lonnie chalked up and broke. They played another game and Lonnie won, playing casually until he was way behind and then rising to the occasion and making shots he had no business making to run the table and win. That was the way it often went. Ed was a steady player and consistent. He took his time and focused and his angles were true. But Lonnie was inspired, not all the time, but in brilliant streaks when the cue seemed to become an extension of his arm and his whole world became the cone of light from the swag lamp hanging over the green felt. If he was right on, Lonnie won, but if he were distracted or his mind drifted, Ed had the advantage and his steady play was enough to win.

They had been drinking Ed's liquor since sundown and they were both breezing along pretty much deadened and oblivious to everything outside the pool hall. Lonnie felt like he was glowing, like he could warm up a room by just walking into it. They kept shooting and drinking, slipping out to Ed's truck between games for a quick swig.

"How's the boy?"

"As good as could be expected."

"You see Janeen?"

"No, and I'm glad I didn't."

"I thought you might want to tell her about Ramona, see if you can drive her crazy jealous."

"I'm not tellin' her. She'll find out soon enough I reckon. Nothin is private 'round here and some busybody is bound to shoot their mouth off. She'll find out. I doubt she'll care."

"You might be surprised."

"If she was to care at all, it'd be for the wrong reasons."

"Well, how about Ramona, what's goin' on there?"

"I like her well enough. She's got a sweet nature but she's tough too."

"I always thought she was a good old girl. Was married before I know but I guess it didn't work out. She came back here after it broke up. Are you all goin' out again?"

"This weekend."

"You old Romeo. Well, what's she like?"

"In bed you mean?"

"Naturally."

"I don't know but I wouldn't tell you if I did. I thought maybe you'd already answered that question for yourself."

"Tried a few times. No luck."

"She's not sure about anything yet. She thinks I'm goin' to run out on her soon as I sell the place."

"Are ya?"

"Probly."

They went back in feeling well oiled and loose and they went to the bar and bought two longnecks. They were discussing whether they should call it an evening or shoot a few more when two of the Maxfield boys came over and asked them if they'd like to play teams and they took them up.

"These old boys can shoot, but they're dumb as posts. Let's take 'em," Ed said.

Ed and Lonnie had achieved a certain level of quality in their pool shooting that evening. The serious shooter knows that to maximize performance, a man has to maintain a precise alcohol buzz. Too little and you have nerves, too much and you're drunk and overconfident. Lonnie and Ed were near that juncture where skill intersects with the perfect buzz. They started mopping up the table with the Maxfield boys. They took the shots they had and when they didn't have a shot they played for position. If they got behind they played defense, setting up impossible leaves for the Maxfield boys to fret over. When they couldn't close out a game the Maxfields became frustrated and started taking it out on the table, smashing the cue ball powerfully, as if to force it to their will. Balls hopped off the table and went bouncing across the pool hall and everyone there looked up to see who had scratched.

They played for a dollar a game and Lonnie and Ed went on a tear and won five games in a row and the Maxfields got real quiet but they kept accepting the rounds of beers Lonnie kept buying with the winnings. The Maxfields won the sixth game and should have had sense enough to quit then but they were encouraged by the win and convinced Lonnie and Ed's winning streak was some kind of fluke so they played on and lost the next three games and ran out of money and had to quit.

They all went out to Ed's truck and he broke out a new jar and they passed it around and soon finished it. It was clear and cold with Orion's belt canted in the southern sky and more stars that could be comprehended and a few fell in bursts of blue-white glory. The air smelled like ice and frost starred the windshield. Ed broke out another quart and they stood around and drank it more slowly and talked about dogs and horses and women.

When they killed that quart Ed proposed driving over to a truck stop at the Arkansas line and having an early breakfast. Lonnie declined feeling a little queasy and not much like traveling or eating. He said goodnight and left Ed and the Maxfields in the lot and he wondered if Ed would be desperate enough to invite the Maxfields to breakfast and buy it for them with their own money. The old truck floated down the highway seemingly having levitated and flew along level a foot off the pavement. He made the turn onto the dirt road and the truck touched down and he listened to the comforting grate of gravel under the wheels. The sky was awash with stars and he turned off the headlights and drove by the baby blue starlight. In the light from the stellar galaxy the road looked silvery and magical and seemed to move around under the truck rocking him gently as if he were back in the womb. In the warmth and darkness of the truck cab he slipped in and out of consciousness.

    He woke up cold and achy and disoriented. His right leg was all twisted up under the steering column and his left leg felt like it wasn't there at all, crammed up against the door and he'd lost circulation in it and it tingled with pin pricks when he flexed it. It was just about first light. He sat up in the truck and looked out across a field to a busted through barbed wire fence and in the muted light he saw two cows standing in the road looking back at him as if they were very pleased with themselves. He knew the spot well. It was on old man Jenkins place where the road curved about two miles from home.
    He got out and looked at the truck and he didn't see any new dents or scratches among the many that marred the body. He looked at the cows. His head felt like a lead weight and his mouth coated and furry and his teeth hurt. For a minute he thought he might throw up and he stood there shivering in the dampness for a while and then he started walking slowly toward the cows. He walked to the road and tried to herd them back through the fence but they were wily and quick and he was cold and lame and sore and he was no match for the contrary beasts.
    As he stood there trying to decide what to do and feeling like just crawling into bed, a new day began, orange light trickling over the horizon. He walked back to the truck and tried it and it started and he drove out of the field over the downed fence and went on home. After starting coffee, he went out and gathered up a few fence posts and some tools and threw them into the truck. In the barn, he put some grain in a bucket and set that in the truck and

then he went back in and poured up the coffee which he drank as he drove back to where the cows were still enjoying their new-found freedom.

He got out the bucket and walked slowly toward the cows and when they looked up at him he poured a little of the grain in the road and stepped back. The cows ambled over and licked up the grain and when they finished the ration they followed him with the bucket back across the flattened fence into the field. While they ate the grain, he got the fence back up, working quickly, skillfully, splicing broken wire, digging out and replacing a broken post, re-stapling the barbed wire in place. In all, it took him about an hour of hard work and the cows were securely enfenced again. A couple of neighbors drove by and he waved and acted like he was just helping out a neighbor whose cows had busted through an old fence and they didn't stop and ask him why he was mending fence at the crack of day but that would have been his story if they had bothered. He drove home feeling poorly in body and slumped into the house and went straight to bed.

He slept the troubled sleep of the day sleeper and woke when shadows were stretching out and the light was oblique to the fields. He stumbled out and went to the kitchen and poured a mug of water and washed down a handful of aspirin. He put on the coffee pot and then went and washed up while it gurgled and steamed. When he went to the closet for fresh clothes he remembered the hawk. He opened the door and pulled out the peach basket but it was empty and he wondered if a critter of some kind had crept in and carried off the dead bird.

A little confounded and not quite yet awake, he began emptying out the closet. He took out several rifles and the old twelve gauge and leaned them against the wall and he leaned an old Louisville slugger beside them. He set out a large family Bible and a shoeshine kit. On all fours he found the sparrow hawk hiding behind a pair of boots at the back of the closet. When it saw him, it flapped off to the corner of the closet and stood there and glared at him. He stood up slowly and closed the closet door and went and poured a cup of strong black coffee and thought some as he sipped at the bitter brew.

When he went back to the closet he had an old hand towel. When he opened the door the hawk stood blinded for a moment, brightly plumed, cobalt blue wings, rufous-capped, white body and head with a black mustache across the face. The hawk made a wobbling run for it and Lonnie threw the towel over it and picked it up wrapping the towel around the body with just the face sticking out of the rolled up towel.

He went to the kitchen and lay the bird on the table and got into the icebox and took out a piece of fresh chicken and sliced off a thin piece and held it out to the hawk. He offered it repeatedly and the hawk ignored it and cowered and then suddenly got the idea or changed its mind and grabbed the chicken and swallowed it. Lonnie sliced off another sliver and the bird took it right away and kept eating until it had consumed half a chicken thigh and then it refused to eat any more. Lonnie lined the peach basket with newspaper and put everything back in the closet including the hawk, releasing it from the towel into the basket just before he shut the door.

He stepped outside to see what the last of the day was like. The sky was orchid, silhouetting the old house against the bright aura and the lighted windows glowed yellow inside the dark outline. Standing there in the front yard as the day closed the house looked homey and comfortable and safe and he suddenly felt he might not like to leave it.

The next day the hawk was noticeably stronger and fought a little longer against being wrapped up in the towel. It readily ate the rest of the chicken thigh and made efforts to bite the hand that fed it. The next day, after another meal, he let it loose in the house and it ran around hiding behind the furniture for a while and settled down for the night on the rung of a kitchen chair. In the following days, the little raptor gained wing strength and began making short flights around the house, perching on light fixtures, curtain rods and on top of the old pie safe. It became more difficult to catch and feed until finally Lonnie got tired of chasing it and just put some raw minced chicken on a saucer on the kitchen table and waited and sure enough the hawk came to it.

The dogs had become aware that another animal was on their turf and they would lean up against the back door and watch the bird eat and sometimes they would get excited and bark at the hawk but the hawk just fired back an angry look through the glass and kept tearing off pieces of chicken.

Two weeks from the day he brought home the hawk was another warm Sunday. That afternoon he propped the front door open and gave the bird a choice. It did not immediately fly out. It looked at the open door for a good long while as if it were considering things and then it dipped in a graceful glide from the light fixture and flitted through the door and flew out and landed in the bare elm tree out front and Lonnie watched it for some time and it just sat there and he wondered if it was strong enough and when he looked out later it was gone.

"What did ya tell 'em?"
"I told 'em no."
"And he offered full price."
"Full price, two-fifty an acre, five thousand even."
"How did they take it?" Ed looked across at Lonnie who was watching Ramona bus a table.
"Not too good I guess. Moore said he had met his contract and

as far as he was concerned I owed him three hundred dollars commission whether I signed the sales contract or not."

"Did you pay up?"

"Hell no. I'm not payin' that tub of guts to stab me in the back. He didn't show the place to a single prospect. He don't deserve nothin'."

"So you takin the place off the market?"

"I might have a few prospects of my own."

"Like who?"

"I don't think I'm goin' to tell ya that."

"How about Looper, old Uncle Henry?"

"He was his usual hateful self. Threatened to take me to court for refusin' to sell to him. Said I was my daddy all over again. I didn't appreciate that and I said a few things maybe I shouldn't of."

"Such as what?"

"Just that the Loopers have been enough of a plague on our family already and I doubt his sister would want him to step foot on the place much less own it. I don't understand how a brother and sister could come from the same mama and papa and be so different. Different as air and dirt. Mama liked the farm life, simple things, having a family. He wouldn't have nothin' to do with her after she married dad. Whole family abandoned her, cut her out of everthin' she was due. She didn't talk about it. Dad told me about it. It's strange havin' relations that are strangers. Worse than strangers, enemies."

"I grew up right down the road from them. Those Loopers always was an uppity bunch but a little strange turned, and old Henry always was just downright mean. He's a kind of man if a rabbit runs out in front of his truck he tries to squash it even if he has to run the truck into the ditch to do it. And he's advised by fairies, he says, little people or somethin' that only he can see and he gets their advice on everthin'. Can you feature that? The rest of them might be a little funny, but old Henry is a real piece of work."

Lonnie looked troubled.

"You probly think I'm crazy to pass, even if he is who he is."

"No more crazy than most."

"You're one to talk."

"I can talk. At least I don't have no Looper blood in me."

"Yeah, you're a real thoroughbred."

A sunny cold day Leonard showed up in his battered blue truck pulling an old single horse trailer. Lonnie helped him unload two scrawny cows into the yard and the two heifers stood in the yard blinking at the brightness of the day and disgruntled. They looked small and young and muscular but their hides and faces were welted with red scratches and they were caked with dirt and they smelled sour and rancid. Lonnie went up to the barn and brought back a bale of alfalfa and busted it up and the animals shuffled over and began ruminating the foliage with enthusiasm. Except for being small for their age and cut up some, they appeared to be healthy.

"Why are they so marked up?"

"Briar patches. They run through 'em all the time. They're half wild."

They had black and white markings and probably carried some Holstein blood, Lonnie thought.

"How many head do you have?"

"I had two. Now I'm out of the ranchin' business."

"But you got horses?"

"A few old ridin' horses, some of 'em out to pasture."

With the help of the dogs they herded the two little cows into the lower pasture and they trotted along just ahead of the dogs belligerently lashing out with a rear hoof occasionally to give the dogs something to think about. The pasture was a little more sheltered and they stood and watched while the cows snuffled and cropped at the sprigs of late winter forage.

They walked back comfortably silent, Leonard looking over the place with new eyes and Lonnie thinking about the many years he and Leonard had trudged and labored in the same fields when his old man had the place waist-high in cotton. Endless sweaty hours he and Leonard had chopped cotton side by side in the summer sun he trying to position his small frame in the large shadow the big Indian cast. Leonard had lived for twenty years in a room in the now tumbled down barn, hanging on until farming went under and he was forced to get a job as a stableman for a rich Cherokee banker.

Lonnie looked back at the cows, now miniature across the distance like the ones in children's barnyard sets. It felt good to have livestock on the place again, even a couple of scrubs. The wind was coming up fresh in his face off the river breaks and the sky was enameled thinly with high layers of clouds and the light was even and true. The hawk was riding the norther hovering almost motionless in the cold blast, wings rocking from the turbulence.

Lost in recounting old history to each other, they walked back up out of the lower pasture, the house appearing above the horizon as they did. A few tiny blue veronica speedwell were heralding the end of the winter and blades of wild irises were sprouting up. They were not far from the house when Lonnie sensed a change in Leonard's demeanor and he looked over to see him looking intently at something. Following his gaze, Lonnie saw the uniformed deputy leaning against the black and white, casually smoking and waiting, papers in hand.

Second date. They went to a chili parlor for a quick bite and then went to see a movie at the old Dream Theater, feeling a little awkward as they sat among a crowd that was mostly high school students and watched a western movie while most of the young couples around them mouthed each other passionately and emitted soft low moans of satisfaction, punctuated with occasional trips to the concession counter.

After the movie they walked over to the Dari Barn arm in arm and had coffee and sundaes, hers hot fudge and his pineapple and they spooned bites into each other's mouths. They lingered a while, sipping coffee and just looking at each other until the chubby high school girl turned off the sign and dimmed the lights and they strolled out into the chill night holding hands.

He awoke to the smell of coffee and frying food and he could tell from the brightness of the curtained window that the day was well started. Dry-mouthed and still groggy, he slipped on the clothes piled on the bedroom chair and pulled on his boots. In the bathroom, he washed his face with cold water and began to wake up. He squeezed out a little toothpaste onto his finger and rubbed down his teeth and then rinsed out, bending over to fill his mouth from the tap. After drying his face on the guest towel, he ran spread fingers through his thinning hair, slicking it back and all these things he did without looking in the mirror.

Ramona stood over her stove, bacon sizzling in the skillet and biscuits in the oven. He stood there watching her and she looked small and fragile and he felt like putting up a wall around her that would shield her from all the hurtful blows life was bound to bring. She must have sensed his presence because she turned and looked at him and gave him a smile and then turned back to her skillet. Lonnie walked up behind her and wrapped his arms around her waist pulling her soft body against his and he stood there soaking in her warmth. She leaned back into him a little and sighed and he could smell her apple scented shampoo and the fresh laundered smell of her bathrobe.

They stood that way for a few heady moments while she finished cooking their breakfast and he liked watching her hands expertly preparing the food, crisping up the bacon, frying the eggs to the perfect tender texture of lightness, browning up golden biscuits, and assembling it on plates.

They sat at the kitchen table and sipped coffee served in cups and saucers matching the plates and they enjoyed the serenity of the Sunday morning and Lonnie kept sneaking sidelong glances at Ramona, noticing things he hadn't seen before, a small mole on her neck, the way her skin was a little more burnished in the webbing between her fingers, the two delicately wrought ridges below her nostrils, a maverick gray hair in her dark mane, the arcing curve of her eyelashes, midnight-black flecks in her wide chestnut eyes.

They used few words, speaking only when a look or gesture would not suffice and using economic phrases when they did say something. He felt comfortable in the snug little kitchen and he wished they could stay there and never leave it and the outside world would just go away. She topped off his coffee and sat down with him at the table and they talked mostly about old times and missed opportunities.

The office smelled like oiled wood and thick carpeting and he could smell the oily odor of the leather sofa on which he waited. A well-dressed secretary was typing up something and he could hear muffled voices from down the hall. He sat clutching his hat and feeling uneasy but mostly he was having trouble shaking off the feeling that he was on a downhill slide that was going to land him somewhere he was unsure of.

The heavy door into the inner sanctum swung open and a tall

old man with a hawk-like face, dressed in an expensive business suit motioned him in, shook his hand firmly, and made small talk. It wasn't long before he spoke seriously.

"I've looked over your case, Mr. Stewart and I'd say we're on sound legal ground. You never signed anything except the listing contract. The law is pretty specific in these instances. If you were being sued by the real estate agent for his commission, I'd say we were in trouble, but that's not the case. Instead Mr. Looper is suing for specific performance, that is to force the sale of your property, and that's very different. The case law is definitely on our side and we can make a very strong case."

"So you're not worried that much?"

"I wish I could say that. As I noted, the law looks good for us. Unfortunately, that's not the end of it. Looper has retained one of the top law firms in the area and even if we win at trial, I'm afraid that will just be the beginning."

"The beginning of what?"

"A protracted court battle, I expect. Let me ask you something, Mr. Stewart. How much money are you willing to spend on this case?"

"All I got, I guess."

"And how much do you think Looper is willing to spend?"

"That old buzzard. You're right. He'll probably hang in until the bitter end. But if I'm winnin' and still livin' on my place, I should be all right. I should be able to ride it out if I've got the law behind me, right?"

"It's not quite that simple. The case could drag on for years in the appellate system and all that time they'll be filing motions, trying to bury us in paper. We'll be forced to respond to their motions, even if they're groundless, and it'll end up costing you more than the value of the property itself. In the meantime, they'll probably get an injunction that keeps you from selling to anyone else until the case is settled. And who knows when that will be, even if you could afford to keep it going."

"But if I managed to pay your legal fees, we could still win on the law?"

"Maybe. Lonnie, I'm going to level with you. You're going to run out of money before they do, and when you're broke, they'll win by default. Even if they didn't have such a financial advantage, well, it's even worse than that. They don't really have much of a case but what they do have is political clout. I hate to tell you this, but I wouldn't be surprised if we lost at trial even though by all rights we should win. You're up against probably the most powerful family in LeFlore County and they're used to getting their way. Hell, Lonnie, I don't have to tell you this. This man is your uncle and I think you know what he's capable of and I know for a fact that these family feuds can be especially nasty."

"He's capable of plenty and he's crooked as a snake. Let me see if I got this right. Old uncle Henry is going to buy a judge so he can swindle me out of my place. Is that how it lays?"

"Technically, it's not a swindle, but yes, in effect, I think he'll try to corrupt the system for his advantage. And I'm sorry to say it's likely he'll be able to do it. Even if he doesn't succeed at the trial level, which he probably will, he may try the same thing with the appeal court. On the face of things, it looks pretty good, but when you consider what's really likely to happen…"

The lawyer raised his hands in a gesture of helplessness.

"I thought I had the right to a jury trial. Wouldn't that put a crimp in their plans?"

"That would probably make it a little more difficult for them, but it probably wouldn't solve things. They'd probably attempt to fix the jury selection process and we'd get to court and find out half the people in the jury pool are Looper plants and even if we fight like hell they'll be able to empanel a jury that's likely to find against you."

"They'll pay off the jury and the judge?"

"Something like that."

"So what should I do? Surely there's somethin'."

The lawyer looked glum.

"Lonnie, I believe you have two options. The first one is to swallow your pride and take the money Looper is offering. It is, after all, the full asking price and since you haven't run up much in legal bills so far, you could walk away with nearly all of it. I didn't ask you why you don't want to sell to him, and I'm not going to, but I'm sure you have good reason for your refusal, whatever it is. But there's something you should ask yourself. Am I willing to sacrifice everything I have over a family grievance? Because that's the second option and in the end you'll probably lose the land anyway, one way or another."

"What would you do?"

"I'm not you, Lonnie, and I don't know what's driving you, but I'd take the money and try to live with it."

Lonnie's face had reddened and a vein in his neck was throbbing rapidly.

"I don't think I can do that. Think I'd rather go the other route."

The lawyer nodded gravely and there was a long moment of silence and the wall clock ticked loudly and cars droned by on the street.

"Why can't we buy us a judge if that's how the game is played?"

The lawyer gave him a sharp look, like a hawk spotting a mouse.

"I can understand how that thought might come to mind. If I responded positively in any way to that idea, I'd be risking disbarment. Realistically, there are some lawyers might be willing to talk to you about it but I doubt you could come up with the kind of cash they'd want and I think you'd probably just end up in a bidding war that sure wouldn't favor you. You're welcome to seek other counsel. It's your right."

Lonnie was stroking the crease into the crown of his hat.

"No, I'll stay with you. You was my daddy's lawyer. You'll be mine too. Just tell me what you think the odds are."

"Of winning?"

"Yeah."

"Even if you costs you the farm?"

"Yeah."

"It's hard to say. Maybe ten to twenty percent. After all your uncle could die or go crazy or change his mind."

"He's already crazy. I can't believe I'm gettin' pushed around by an old man who sees little green men and treats his own blood like stepchildren. But you say we ain't got much of a chance."

"If it was a horse, it would be a long shot."

"But you're willin' to go into court and lose if that's what I want?"

"It's your money and your decision."

"Then if we go down, let's go down fightin'."

"I'd be proud to represent you."

Lonnie stood up and walked over and shook the old lawyer's hand and turned to go. The lawyer looked thoughtful.

"There is one thing you could do."

Lonnie paused, looking back.

"If you could find out why it is your uncle wants your place so bad, that might give us an edge. There must be something going on for him to engage in a legal battle. I'm sure he knows you're not weak-willed. You have any thoughts on that?"

"Other than pure oneriness, I ain't got a clue"

"Think some on it. You're uncle's a crotchety old man, but he's not insane. I wonder what he's up to."

"Lord knows. It's beyond me."

"Well, watch your step, and say hello to your dad for me next time you visit."

"Thank ya kindly. I appreciate it."

When he got home the two cows were gone and it didn't take long to find the weak spot in the fence. They cows had found a rotten post and snapped it off at ground level and trampled down the wire and headed out. He tracked their escape route, which paralleled the river, for about an hour until the light began to fade and his leg began pulsing like a live wire and he turned around and slowly tramped back in the dark.

The next morning broke gray and cold with low-hanging leaden clouds spitting rain and a rising wind whipping up out of the north. Homer rode in on a little sorrel cutting horse about an hour after first light leading old Buster and holding his hat to keep it from blowing away. They put the horses in the ramshackle old barn which looked like the wind might blow it over at any moment and slipped into the house for a cup of hot coffee before riding out.

It took them four miserable hours to find the maverick cows and another two to drive them back and put the fence back up. The cows were miles downriver, in a little sidehill stand of post oaks, seeking shelter from the weather. Homer went after them on the little cutting horse and the cows bolted uphill and the chase was on. Lonnie followed along at a lope on old Buster. The cows were scrambling up the rocky slope wildly but they were no match for the horse which gained quickly on them, flanked them within fifty yards or so and turned them back down the slope and by the time they broke out of the timber into the meadow along the river, the cows were tired and allowed themselves to be herded back upriver with no difficulty.

As the cold front moved in, it became colder, windier and wetter. Their slickers and hats provided some protection, but the wind was blowing the rain sideways into their faces and it ran down inside their collars until their shirts were soaked and the wind swirled up under the slickers ballooning them up around their waists while cold water soaked their jeans and ran down into their boots until the boots filled with rainwater and they had to shuck their feet out of the stirrups and extend their legs forward and point their toes to drain them. The clouds lowered appearing to hang just over the treetops and sleet mixed with the rain and coated their slickers with a shell of ice.

It was late in the afternoon when they got back to the house, soaked to the skin and numb with cold. By the time they unsaddled and dried off the horses and gave them a generous ration of grain, the day was dimming out. The ground was being encapsulated in ice beads as they crunched across he hardening ground between the barn and the house and the wind was coming in gusts blowing ice pellets in a stinging volley into their faces, quickening their steps. Inside, Lonnie stoked up the fire and they stood around the glowing stove steaming and dripping and sniffing for a few minutes and then they both stripped naked, toweled off and basked in the waves of warmth from the roaring fire and Homer fired up a Winston and sucked at it appreciatively.

Lonnie got them a couple of quilts and they draped themselves in togas and stood around the stove feeling a tingling burn in their toes and fingers as the blood returned and passing a quart jar of brew back and forth. After a while Lonnie went in the kitchen and put a pot of beans on to warm and set out a pan of cold cornbread. He pulled a smoked ham out of the icebox and sliced off four thick slabs and put them in a pan in the oven. While he was waiting for the food to get warm he rejoined Homer by the stove.

"Old Buster did all right out there today."

"For a seventeen-year-old. Your little horse did all the work."

"He's sure a good un. Those little heifers didn't have a chance."

"They're an onery pair. You reckon you could let old Buster stay on here a few days just in case they bust out again."

"Sure, he'll probably enjoying visitin' his old stompin' grounds. You know I still can't believe you let him go."

"I got no place for him after I sell out. You treat your horses like pets. He's better off with you I reckon."

"Wasn't he a birthday present or somethin'?"

"Graduation. Dad gave him to me and he weren't no more than a skinny colt just weaned from his mom. First few months I had him I practically lived out in the barn."

"I'm not sure I could give up a horse like that." Homer looked into his face and Lonnie had a far-off expression and didn't say anything for a long moment.

"Cuz, you'd be surprised what you can give up."

The sleet storm turned out to be the demarcation between winter and spring. The melting ice brought up wildflowers. Blue veronicas, pink spring beauties and purple wood violets splashing the ground like draps of bright paint. He rode the fencelines on old Buster, testing old posts for sturdiness, tightening up wire, pounding in new staples. The little cows stayed home and seemed content in the verdant lower pasture and began to put on some weight and look healthier.

He drank less and sat out on the porch in the cool of the evening and listened to the high-pitched trills of tree frogs and the singing of crickets who seemed to scratch out their song for the sheer joy of it. Within weeks the nightly chorus was enriched by a whippoorwill calling across the distance plaintively. He could smell the greening grass on the moist wind that blew up from the pasture and he was having second thoughts about everything he thought he was so sure about. Still he found many things about his life tedious but he also came to realize that there were things that would be lost to him that he would miss painfully.

The spring nights reminded him of when his dad would take an old mattress and throw it down in the yard and they would lie on it in the early evening, he between his mom and dad, and they would have a contest to see who could find the first star to come out and they would always let him find it as it magically appeared from the black slate of the firmament. They would watch until the sky was salted with flashing stars and steadily shining planets and before he would fall asleep he would always see a few falling stars blaze a silver trail across the celestial dome, dying gloriously.

One night he lit an old coal oil lamp to enjoy the soft glow of golden light it gave the living room and he lay on the couch in his skivvies watching moths, some as big as his hand flutter against the screen. Through the frame of the screen he watched the moon rise orange as cheese through the haze and getting smaller as it tracked slantwise up the doorway paling and shrinking until it was a pearl pouring forth blue light on the fields and smudging out the stars.

He was thinking of Ramona when the phone rang and thought he must have intuited a call from her and he picked it up eagerly by the second ring, but it was not Ramona at all.

The old truck rattled across the long bridge and he could see the Arkansas flat and muddy and slow moving down below. The bridge ended where Garrison Avenue the wide main drag of Fort Smith began. He drove by old Judge Parker's courthouse and gallows from the old west days where outlaws had been hanged in bunches. Mid-morning light saturated the red brick storefronts and people bustled around energized by multiple cups of coffee. He rumbled the few blocks to the federal building and found a parking place on the street.

He consulted the building directory in the marble-lined lobby and walked up the stairs to the jail where he waited to talk to a marshal behind a huge oak counter who didn't seem to be doing much but wouldn't look up and acknowledge his presence. Finally he did and he inquired about posting bond for Ed and the marshal told him to wait and went through a gray metal door that had a window that was reinforced with wire net. He was gone a long time, some of which he could see through the window was taken up by a gregarious conversation and coffee break with a co-worker. Finally he returned to say that Ed was still being processed and it would be a few hours before he could be released. He wondered what being processed consisted of, but he didn't ask and he didn't want to wait in the depressing atmosphere of the jail so he went out to walk the streets.

He walked around, window shopping for an hour or so, just killing time and his stomach commenced growling and he remembered he had skipped breakfast in his urgency to get to Fort Smith and he started looking for a place to eat. He found a diner on a side street that advertised home made pies and it was packed with workers on their lunch hour but he managed to seat himself at the one small table that was available, still stacked with dirty dishes from the previous party. The waitress came and cleared the plates and picked up her tip and wiped off the table top with a damp rag and he had looked over the menu by then and ordered coffee and a chicken fried steak plate lunch and hoped it would come soon.

It did and he tore into it with a hearty appetite. He was so ravenous and savoring his lunch so much that he did not notice the tall man standing over his table until the man spoke asking him if he could join him as all the other tables were full. Sit on down, he said looking the man over as he pulled out the chair and lowered himself into it. Middle-aged, well groomed with a big handlebar mustache wearing a white dress shirt and a black string tie. The man introduced himself but he could not quite catch the name in the loud lunchtime café chatter as they shook hands across the table.

The man caught the eye of a waitress as she scurried by and ordered the roast beef plate lunch and an iced tea. By the time the roast beef came, Lonnie had finished his food and the waitress poured him another cup of coffee and he ordered a piece of the home-made apple pie. They fell into conversation, the way strangers will when they are thrown together in a chance encounter. Lonnie didn't tell him why he was in town but he did admit to being an Okie from LeFlore County and he thought he saw a bemused look on the man's face for a moment and it irritated him that even Arkansawyers looked down on his native state.

But overall the man was jovial and a good conversationalist and Lonnie learned that he worked out of the same federal building he had already visited that morning. They ended up walking back over to the building together and when they got into the lobby the man said, "Come on into my office for a minute."

He worked for the Army Corps of Engineers, or at least that's what was painted on the door leading into a suite of offices. The man had a big corner office with windows looking down across the business section to the river. Maps covered tables and desks and a drafting table stood against the interior wall.

"How are you at keeping secrets Mr...."

"Stewart, Lonnie Stewart. I can keep my mouth shut if I've a mind to I guess."

"You're gonna need to do that Lonnie because I'm fixin' to show you something that not too many folks know about and I think it might concern you."

The man was riffling through some large maps and he pulled one out big as a card table and laid it out on his desk.

"Take a look at this and see if this looks familiar to you."

Lonnie stared at the chart getting oriented to north and south and he began to see roads and streams and little towns in LeFlore County and he found the dirt road out to his place and the topographical landmarks he knew so well on his land. Squarely across the middle of his plot a sinuous blue line snaked across the map and continued onto old man Jenkins place. Where his house sat a black rectangle marked the spot.

"What's the blue line mean?"

"That's the lake."

"There ain't no lake."

"Not yet there isn't."

Comprehension stunned him and he remembered the vague rumors he had heard about the federal boys sniffing around and looking and driving around in gray pick-ups with government license plates.

It comes right across my place he said pointing to the black rectangle.

"Looks like you own some lake-front property, or you will in a few years. And that black rectangle, that's the planned project office."

He had to wait around until the middle of the afternoon until Ed appeared before a judge who would set his bail. Two beefy marshals brought Ed into the courtroom in handcuffs and leg shackles like he was a dangerous outlaw. The judge set bail at twenty-five hundred, more money than Lenora had given him and he had to go out and find a bail bondsman and give him two hundred and fifty dollars to bond Ed out. Finally amid rush hour traffic they headed home.

Ed told him how he had gone over to Arkoma to do some business with one of his regulars and was approached by two men he didn't know who talked him into selling them a jar. They turned out to be treasury agents and they hauled him off to Fort Smith where he had spent the night in jail.

"Why'd you sell to 'em if you didn't know 'em?"

"I wished the hell I hadn't but they looked all right. They had scraggly hair and beards, tore up old clothes and mud on their boots. Appeared like Arkies to me."

"How'd they get on to you in the first place?"

"Somebody must of run off at the mouth."

Ed shook his head mournfully and fired up a Pall Mall and they rolled along quietly for a while. Lonnie was thinking hard about the new knowledge he had acquired but he didn't tell Ed because keeping confidences was not in his nature. It would be all over the county in a matter of days if he shared it with Ed.

Still he felt sorry for him and it was of the rare times he had seen his friend so gloomy and quiet.

"So you think you can wiggle out of this one?"

"Don't know. It's a federal rap. May be more serious."

"So what you gonna do?"

"May do some time, not much I hope."

"Good lawyer might get you off. They know the ins and outs."

"Probly just screw me out of some money and sell me down the river."

"'Fraid you might be right. Gotta be somethin' you can do though."

"I could run off but I'm not gonna. I tell you what drives me crazy though. Big whisky distillery turns out a river of sour mash and nobody cares. But if I try to make a few dollars doin' the same thing they want to thow me in the joint."

"Ain't right is it?"

"This country is so bass ackwards. Folks know it too. Cops are the most hated people around and Pretty Boy Floyd is a hero for robbin' banks."

"Hope you don't end up like him."

"I don't aim to bro, that's for sure. You got anything to drink in here?"

"I'm not that stupid. Could get some beer."

Ed snorted and lit a new unfiltered off the butt of the previous one and then tossed the butt out and it made an orange shower of sparks hitting the pavement in the early twilight.

"It'd take a case and a half before I could even feel it. Let's find us a bootlegger."

"Lenora's probly wonderin' what the hell's goin' on."

"Lenora always expects the worst, and she usually gets it. Oh hell, take me on home."

"I wish I had better news I really do."

He was once again sitting across the desk from his father's lawyer, now his. The lawyer opened a manila folder turned a document around and laid it in front of him.

"It's called a summary judgment. If the presiding judge finds it's an open and shut case no matter what evidence exists, he can rule for one party without a trial. The judge found for your uncle without even giving us a day in court."

It felt like all the air had been drained out of his chest. He looked at the paper in front of him the way he would look at a dead animal repeatedly run over in the road. It felt like pressure was building inside his skull.

"You mean we lost before we even got started? What a chickenshit deal."

"Couldn't agree more. It ignores all the case law to say nothing of your rights under the Fourteenth Amendment. The judge ruled that your signature on the listing agreement comprised a valid sales contract provided the buyer was willing to pay the full asking price. But that's not the worst of it. The judge issued an order directing the county registrar of deeds to transfer title of your property thirty days after the full asking price is placed in escrow with the court. This morning a deputy brought this over."

The lawyer took another item out of the folder and placed it on top of the court order. It was a certified check made out to Lonnie for five thousand dollars.

"Whether you accept the check or not, title will transfer a month from today."

"What if I refuse to go?"

"Then you'll be forcibly removed by the sheriff and, knowing how this might go, probably shot and maybe killed, depending on how much they've been paid by your uncle and what he wants to happen."

The phone rang and the lawyer grabbed it up roughly and said, "No calls now, I don't care who it is," and he whapped the receiver back into the cradle.

"This is one of the worst railroadings I've seen in all my days of practicing law. The judge that wrote out this order lives in a house that might be the biggest in this county. He built it while serving on the bench at the appointed salary of six thousand dollars a year. But it's been common knowledge for a long time that if you want something done your way in court, a few thousand will fix it. Say you need your old mom declared incompetent so you can get you hands on her property. Say you lost it momentarily and killed somebody who wasn't really important anyway. Say you steal some cattle or get caught in bed with a fourteen-year-old. You pony up, you ride out of town with things your way. It's always been that way. It probably always will."

Lonnie stared at the thick carpet in stunned silence. He didn't know what to say or where to start.

"Ain't there anything?" He could hear the flag flapping across the street at the courthouse in the pregnant pause before the old lawyer answered.

"We could appeal to the Oklahoma Supreme Court."

"Could we get this tossed out if we did?"

"I believe we probably would. I doubt the Supreme Court would ignore precedent the way the district court did. But it would be a year or more before they heard the case and even if they threw out this judgment, they'd most likely order a new trail be conducted and, guess what, we'd be right back at square one, only a year or so would of gone by during which they would be in possession and control of your land. And if we proceeded to a new trail, guess what judge would still be presiding over the case? The same son of a bitch who's already bought and paid for."

"Can't win for losin'."

Lonnie looked forlorn.

"What would you do?"

"Honestly? I wouldn't be so much worried about what to do as I was about what they might do to me. Let me tell you a story. It won't help any but let me tell it anyway.

"It's about my papa. He was the first representative sent to the state legislature from LeFlore County when Oklahoma became a state in 1907. Then in 1912 he was elected state senator for the next sixteen years. When I was about twelve, he began letting me go around with him and I'd spend my day at his office in the state capitol. He'd been in office a long time by then and he had a nice suite of offices.

"I'd stay in the outer office with his secretary and a whole string of visitors would come by every day to talk with papa. Before they went in, they dropped off an envelope with the secretary. Those envelopes didn't have much in them by today's standards, twenty dollars, fifty, a hundred, but over the course of a legislative session they added up. Most of the people came more than once and many came by several times a month. I sat out in the lobby and watched the parade of pitchmen and at the end of the day, papa slipped the envelopes into his pocket. I was only twelve, but I understood exactly what was going on.

"It was everybody you could imagine and a lot you couldn't coming through the door every day. Oil company lobbyists in droves. Timber company people. Highway contractors, textbook companies, furniture suppliers. That might be one typical day."

A sardonic grin creased the lawyer's face.

"Shouldn't be surprised. The whole U.S. of A. is up for sale. Will Rogers said it best. 'We have the best politicians money can buy'. He was talking about Congress, but he might as well have been talking about LeFlore County. But I do think, based on what I knew about papa, that Oklahoma is the only state where crookedness was built into the system right from statehood. It's been there for fifty years now and by god if most people don't think it's a tradition we should continue as part of who we are. The good old boy system and I don't see any sign it's going away."

"More like the rich old boy system I reckon."

The lawyer spoke slowly, warmly, as to a grandchild.

"I expect you sort of knew that in the back of your mind. This is a hard choice, but five thousand could be enough to make a nice new start, maybe say, about a month down the line. Your goal was to sell the farm and leave. The first part's done. I hope you carry through on the second part. I don't like it much being jerked around but I recommend you stick that check in your pocket and walk out of here for good."

Lonnie scooted forward and pressed his hat on.

"I'll think about it. You keep it for now."

Next morning. He woke at first light to the call of redbirds and he lay there a while watching the light go from ochre to cream and finally he rolled out and wandered into the kitchen and put on some coffee. After washing up, he stood on the front porch with a scalding mug of black brew and sipped at it slowly. It was one of those spring days that had the fresh smell of new growth mixed with wildflowers, borne on a cool but moist breeze, vernal, unmistakable. Down across the fields the cows had their heads down to the meadow and a small herd of deer stood against the forest wall on the far side of the waving grasses. He stood there transfixed with the view and finished the bitter coffee and then he went into the bedroom and took out the old Colt six-gun.

He went out and saddled up old Buster and had a second mug and then rode away from the river, up into the hills, through white stands of dogwood, each propeller-like petal tinged at the tip the color of dried blood. The legend of the dogwood came from his mother, who said the dogwood once had blooms of pure white, but that when Jesus was crucified, the tips of the dogwood petals were stained to the color of His blood, to symbolize the four wounds with which he was attached to the cross.

The trees were leafing out in the lime green of new growth interspersed with the magenta foliage of redbuds and white clad wild plum. May apple was springing up and trout lilies grew beside the old outlaw trail he rode through the hills. Once he stopped where water welled up from the rocky hillside at the base of a bluff and a freshet splashed off down the terrain. Ferns framed the spring and watercress grew in the sandy shallows. He and old Buster drank deeply and he splashed the cold water on his face and he let the old horse rest a while before riding on.

It began to get warmer and even under the canopy of the leafing-out trees he and the horse started to sweat and soon the back of his shirt was wet and stuck to his spine. Old Buster walked slowly but steadily, willingly. Finally, they stood on a windswept limestone escarpment jutting from a steep wooded hillside. Down across the flats at the base of the hills, tucked in nicely with a little stream flowing by, stood his uncle's house, a big barny saltbox wrapped with wide covered porches. A big shiny car beamed back the morning brightness.

He saw no activity but he rode on down, old Buster sure footed among the scattered litter of rockfall and eroded out scree. They crossed the flat, Buster's hooves clopping on the packed ground and he tied the old horse to a fence post and walked up a worn path toward the front porch. In the middle of the front yard he stopped, pulled the old Colt from his belt and fired it into the air three times.

His uncle pulled the door open and blinked at him and stuck out his jaw. His skin was yellowed to the color of old newspaper and his pale blue eyes were rheumy and tired. A leathery wattle hung above his Adam's apple and the mottled skin stretched across the top of his head made him looked skeletal.

"What the hell do you want?"

"I come to tell you I'm not movin' off. You'll have to shoot me."

"You think I won't? I've eaten bigger men than you for breakfast."

"Why don't ya then? I'm trespassin' on your property ain't I?"

His uncle spat hard in anger toward him and the oxblood sputum splattered halfway between them.

"I believe I will. You wait right there while I get my deer rifle."

The door slammed shut. He stood there waiting, listening for the old goat's returning footsteps to approach the door, straining for his footfalls. He waited with a heightened sense of awareness of how much he wanted to get back on his horse and ride off and go home and have a third mug of coffee. He waited while a mockingbird made the rounds through the bushes in the yard singing a medley of calls. He waited while a cloud crossed the sun. Finally, when he had almost decided that his uncle was not coming back, the brittle old man hobbled slowly onto the porch, dwarfed by the big game rifle he held at the ready. He took a stance at the top of the porch steps and leveled the rifle at Lonnie who raised the revolver in response.

They stood there like duelists squaring off, glaring down the sights at each other. Lonnie's eyes locked on the end of the deer rifle, which wavered in little circles in his uncle's palsied hands. Lonnie squinted down the barrel of the heavy Colt, aiming at the opening in the end of the rifle's barrel, as if he could shoot and intercept the lead in flight when the rifle fired. Or maybe he could shoot the rifle out of old Henry's hands, movie cowboy style. Then, before he saw a flash, or heard a report, or saw smoke curl from the barrel of the thirty-thirty, Lonnie hurled backwards into blackness.

Part III

Feathers Fly

    Most afternoons, he would stop by the café after the lunch crowd had cleared out and Ramona would take a break and they would sit in a booth and pass the time together talking pleasantly. The bullet had plowed a groove in the side of his head, along the temple. He wore a white gauze bandage, shaped like a turban, and Ramona was solicitous of his every need, plying him with all manner of drinks and desserts as well as radiating warmth and affection on him.

    It would have felt right if things had not been going so wrong, but he kept his troubles to himself and though it was mildly dishonest, and he felt uneasy about it, he did not share with her the impending deadline he faced to clear off, nor the lake. It was not that she could not be trusted. She could. It was that he did not want to burden her or ruffle the way things were and he knew she would be alarmed and saddened by the facts at hand.

One quiet weekday afternoon an old man walked in and sat down at the counter. From his appearance he could have been a professional hobo in off the Kansas City Southern or a drifter down on his luck and looking for a handout. Then Lonnie recognized him as the old coot he had given a ride home out close to Shady Point.

Ramona scooted out and carried a glass of ice water over to him where he sat hunched over in as close to a fetal position as could be maintained on a stool. In a low voice, he ordered a piece of pie and she brought it and set it in front of him and then rejoined Lonnie in the booth.

They sat there mostly looking at each other while dishes clattered in the kitchen as they were washed and put away. She noted that he looked skinnier and tried to interest him in an early dinner but he declined saying he would rather just sit with her for a while. The old man appeared to have gone to sleep. He sat like a lump, still, head down, pie untouched. Ramona got up to check on him.

"Is there somethin wrong with that pie hon?"

He looked up with watery bloodshot eyes.

"How much is the pie?"

"A quarter."

"How much for a hamburger?"

"A quarter."

"If you don't mind, I think I'd like to trade that pie for a hamburger."

"Sure thing." She lifted the pie off the counter and put it back in the glass pie case.

She waited around wiping up until the order came up and brought it still steaming from the grill and plunked it down and refilled his water glass.

This time, the man did not hesitate. He grabbed the burger

with both hands and consumed it in big hungry satisfied bites. Ramona sat down again.

When he was finished, he wiped off his mouth and stood and walked casually toward the door. His hand was on the doorknob when Ramona spoke.

"Mister, you forgot to pay for your hamburger."

He stood there looking as calm and thoughtful as a man in mismatched rumpled clothing can manage to look.

"Don't you remember, miss? I traded you that piece of pie for the burger." He turned to go.

"Wait a minute. You didn't pay for the pie neither."

"Why, I didn't eat the pie, miss," and he pushed the door open and walked out.

Ramona had moved toward the register a few steps in anticipation of receiving payment and when the man walked out she was at first flabbergasted and then amused and then she bubbled with laughter.

Lonnie offered to pay the man's bill, but she said no and pulled a quarter out of her tips and rang it up.

The call came as he was having morning coffee. His sister gave him the news. The old folks home had called. It was over. Found by a housekeeper. The body already moved to the funeral home.

"I'll come," Lonnie said.

He chose a silver and blue casket and signed up for a time payment plan. Redwine let him take some boxes and he went to the home and packed up his dad's things. Among the clothes, he found the old blue serge Sunday suit, a white shirt, a navy tie and black cowboy boots, and set them aside to take to the funeral home.

The other old man in the room was withdrawn, sullen, and looked at Lonnie with a fierce gaze, like Lonnie had no right to be messing with another man's property. His father's bed was stripped and very empty. In the pocket of a jean jacket, Lonnie found twenty-year-old ticket stubs to the Old Fort Days rodeo. There were jeans molded to the shape of the old man's knees. An old cardboard suitcase he remembered from a family vacation to Colorado.

The new blonde nurse came in and gave him a small bag. Glasses, dentures, and a wedding ring.

"I'm sorry for your loss, Mr. Stewart. I liked your father. Sometimes he'd look at me and smile when I came in here. He asked me one time if I was his daughter."

"Thank for the kind words. Can you tell me anything about the end?"

"I wasn't here. But I heard he was just fine one minute and gone the next. A woman came in to clean the room and noticed he wasn't breathing. It happens that way sometimes."

"So you don't think he suffered?"

"I don't think so."

"You know, it's not death so much that scares me. It's the dyin'."

"I know what you mean. There are good ways to die and terrible ways. Your father's was a good one."

"Thanks for taking care of him. I'm going to get these boxes out."

"Guess I won't be seeing you anymore."

Lonnie looked at her and she looked back.

"Guess not." He stacked two boxes and carried them out.

His sister's house filled with kinfolks the day of the service, the kitchen filled with food until the counters and table could hold no more. It had the festive air of a family reunion, and the solemn atmosphere of a church, somehow combined. Relatives unseen for years drove in from across the state. Cars and trucks stretched up and down the street and neighbors showed up at the door with pies, cakes and casserole dishes.

Larry, Janeen and Clay were waiting in the Lincoln outside the Baptist church. They got out when they saw Lonnie and Clay strode across the gravel lot looking uncomfortable in a new charcoal three-piece suit and black cowboy boots. Clay had a hurt look on his face and didn't say anything. Lonnie put his arms around his shoulders and they walked together toward the door.

Lonnie and Clay sat at the front of the church with his sister and her family. The old preacher said some words about what a fine man his father had been. The mortician had used too much make-up and his dad looked ruddy, like he had just come in from the cold, when, in fact, he was headed into it. The blue suit and the gleaming blue casket matched nicely. Smiling benevolently, the preacher told a story about how his father had once given away a team of mules to a neighbor whose mules had drowned. His sister sobbed softly and her husband put his arm around her shoulders. At the end, the choir sang *Shall We Gather at the River.*

Lonnie and his sister rode in a limousine to the cemetery, familiar landmarks made strange by the surreal nature of the experience. Mid-afternoon of a late spring day, the world clad in a new green coat, they stood around the grave three deep and the preacher read from the Bible about ashes and dust. Lonnie's throat swelled and he stood there holding his hat, feeling helpless. A sweet breeze out of the south bent the grasses, the light was pure and white, and clouds sailed across a sea of sky. On such a day, it didn't feel right to put someone in the ground. It should be storming, or cold and gray, or cloudy and gloomy.

They left him there in the fancy box, poised over the grave and rode away in the big black limo. When Lonnie looked back he saw the gravediggers walking slowly toward the bier, getting ready to perform the final act.

Lenora opened the weather-beaten door and gave him a look that said, "Oh, it's you and what do you want as if I didn't know." She could say a lot with a look.

"He's out back."

She shut the door quickly before he could get turned around and scuff across the creaky cupped boards and down the steps. He walked around back and down the hill past purple spiderwort and found Ed leaning against a post watching the hogs. Ed nodded.

"You ever seen the likes of this?"

Lonnie joined him at the fence. Most of the hogs lay in repose scattered around the pen, some of them snoring. He had never heard hogs snoring before. One hog tried to struggle onto its legs, wobbled along a few steps and fell heavily over onto its side. Another hog was scooting along on its belly, two were asleep with their chins still in the trough and an old sow was lying on her back with all four legs pointed straight up.

"What's wrong with 'em? They sick or somethin'?"

"They're drunk as skunks, ever one of 'em."

"How'd that happen?"

"I fed 'em two drums of mash. First I reckoned they'd have trouble finishin' it but they did. Kinda reminds me of when I was younger. They look right peaceful though don't they?"

"What possessed ya?"

"I told ya I was goin' to use more caution. Goverment pickup drove by real slow a while ago. Two men in gray shirts, looked like some kind of laws, not local, that's fer sure, goverment plates and all. Took a good look over the place and one of 'em pointed out somethin' before they drove off. I had a batch brewin', just about ready to burn off, so I rushed down here and tried to figure out how to best be shed of it. The hogs took care of it just fine."

"Truck ever come back by?"

"No, but I ain't taken no chances these days. Got enough problems as it is."

They stood there a while and studied the hog pen. The hog that had been trying to walk around started heaving like it might throw up. Lonnie shook his head.

"Hog can't hold his liquor. Maybe you ought to make up a barrel of coffee."

"How about I just put a pot on for us?"

"Sounds like a plan." They walked back up toward the house together. Ed seemed a little subdued.

"You work out that little problem you had?"

"Might of. I'm still considerin' things. They offered a deal if I plea."

"What kind of a deal?"

"Six months free room and board, out in three on good behavior."

"You gonna take it?"

"Probly."

"When?"

"A few weeks, a month, whenever I make up my mind for sure."

"No way you can walk?"

"Not hardly. They got an airtight case against me they say. We go to trial, lawyer wants two thousand. Cheaper to do the three months."

Lonnie stared at the toes of his boots. A mockingbird practiced several different calls. He needed a drink.

"Got anything?"

"No shine. Got some bootleg though."

They laced the coffee with good Tennessee sour mash and sat out on the back steps and tried to catch up with the hogs.

He woke suddenly rising to the surface of consciousness like a swimmer from underwater dizzy for that first sweet gulp of air. The dogs were upset over something, but the dogs raised the alarm over most anything, a passing skunk, a possum. Then he heard the chickens and he knew someone or something was out there. He rolled out and pulled on some jeans and grabbed the old twelve gauge out of the closet. He eased out the back door into an overcast moonless night and stood there letting his eyes adjust to the dark.

The chickens had settled down and the dogs were trotting around officiously like they were satisfied that they had things under control. He stood there relying more on his ears than his eyes and he could hear old Buster nicker in the barn and a barn owl screeched from the trees along the river. Other than that, all was quiet. He was getting ready to turn around and go in when he heard a car start down on the road and roar off with no headlights.

He went in and got the flashlight and went around to the barn, the chicken house, the front yard. Everything seemed to be as it should. The dew was cold against his bare feet and he was fully awake now and spooked by the lonesome hour of the night and the damp impenetrable darkness. He flashed the beam over the old truck and counted up the dogs following him around the yard. Nothing amiss. He went back to bed but had trouble going to sleep, fading into a restless doze when gray light seeping over the horizon banished the darkness.

It was the next afternoon before he found the dead cows. The clouds had cleared and the day turned off pretty. Sitting out on the porch eating a fried baloney sandwich for lunch it struck him that not only could he not see the cows grazing down in the pasture, but that he had not seen them all morning. The cows had broken out and bolted the fence again was his first thought and when he finished eating he went out to the barn and saddled up old Buster in anticipation of having to once again chase them down.

Instead, he found them lying in the sun already bloating up. He dismounted to take a closer look. They had both been shot, one squarely between the eyes, slaughterhouse style. The other one had apparently fled and was shot twice, once in the shoulder and another shot which had struck the little heifer in the neck and pierced the jugular. A brownish red circle of dried blood clumped in the fresh grass where the animal had bled to death. Old Buster snorted and dragged on the reins and he stumbled backwards and almost fell down.

He felt the blood surge to his face and his jaw jutted out in outrage. He spat a wad of phlegm out forcefully and muttered curses against the shooter and then against the person who sent the shooter. Why had he slept through the shots? Why didn't he pursue the car he heard drive away? What was there to do now? He stood in the sun head down and churned inside. Old Buster pushed his nose against his back.

He took some of the anger out on the earth, taking the rest of the afternoon to dig a pit by hand, stabbing at the ground until he stood waist deep in it. Sweat soaked his shirt, his neck reddened, his eyes burned from salty trickles off his scalp. He ached from the effort, flinging out red earth until it piled head-high, digging out rocks, the wind whipping dirt into his face.

Toward sundown, his body began to run down and the interrupted night of sleep began to take a toll. The wind went down and cool crept up from the river and the whole scene was bathed in golden light. It was getting dark in the hole. Sun on the horizon, he climbed out and went over and caught old Buster. The old horse was no cutter, but he knew enough to dally and he hitched one end of the rope to the saddlehorn and looped the other end around the neck of the first carcass and he took the reins and led in the right direction and Buster strained and dragged the dead cow into the pit. He repeated the procedure and dropped the second cow into the hole.

His muscles felt rubbery and he felt like his knees might buckle. His leg was singing in pain. He filled the grave, mounding up the extra dirt and stomping it down and by the time he finished the light was gone and he dragged himself up on the horse by sheer willpower and rode back to the house holding the shovel across the cantle. He still had to see to the horse and feed the animals.

Food didn't interest him, but he was parched and drank dipper after dipper of cool well water. He didn't care if he was dirty and encrusted with salty residue and smelled. He sat out on the front porch jangled, numb, and stiff. He could not hear the whippoorwills crying out to each other, nor see the shining planets rising over the mist.

He badly wanted a drink, but there was nothing in the house and he was soured on the human race as a whole and wanted to see no one. The dogs hung close and he realized he had not fed them and he dragged himself up and took care of them. After that he went out and lay down on his back on the porch and it was there that exhaustion drove him into the sweet blissful ignorance of sleep.

"You coulda told me, I woulda understood."

Somehow she had found out about the court order and the dead cows and the connection between them. It was hard to keep secrets in a small town.

"I wanted to tell ya but it woulda wore on ya so I kept it to myself. Too bad more people can't keep their mouths shut. I guess everbody in the county knows by now."

"No, I think there's an old hermit way back in the sticks don't know it yet."

They were parked outside the VFW hall getting ready to go in to the Saturday night dance. Couples crossed the gravel parking lot walking bouncily along in anticipation of a good time.

"Lonnie, can I ask you somethin' kinda…personal?"

"Go ahead."

"Don't get mad on me now."

"Uh-huh."

"All right then, don't take this wrong or nothin', but are you sure you're over Janeen? I mean it really hasn't been that long since your breakup and I know it hurt you real bad. I don't believe a person usually gets over something like that for a long time."

Lonnie folded his arms and thought for a minute.

"This ain't my favorite subject."

"All right, if you don't want to talk about it you don't have to. It's not my business."

Lonnie studied the parking lot where a cop car was prowling through.

"Don't you take this wrong neither, but I don't know if I'll ever get over it." He paused and weighed his words.

"I thought I knew Janeen, but I guess I didn't know her at all. I didn't even see it comin'. She had this other person hid inside her, somebody different. One day that other person took over and that was it. That's about all I know. So, yeah, I guess I'm damaged goods if that's what you're getting at."

"We're all damaged goods Lonnie."

"Maybe, but some more than most."

"I don't think of you that way. I don't think most people that know you do either."

"That don't really matter to me."

"Sure it matters. If you was no count, that'd be one thing, but I know that ain't it."

"Bein' a good person don't account for near as much as I oncet thought. Bad things happen to good people all the time and good things happen to bad people. Sometimes I think that life is sorta like a pinball machine. We go bouncing around, ringing bells and making lights flash, and it's real excitin', but it don't last, never does. And the ball always ends up bein' lost."

"Well, maybe you just enjoy the fun while you can. Maybe everthing's temporary as a soap bubble."

"Yeah, maybe, but it's more'n that. Life ain't just tricky, it's plum contrary."

"A person can't spend their whole life feeling sorry."

"Yes they can, Ramona, yes they can."

"Well, it's a waste of a life."

"Most lives are mostly waste I reckon."

"Maybe some, maybe a lot of them, but it don't have to be that way, not for everbody."

"I don't think I want to talk about this anymore and I'm afraid I aint got the answers you want to hear."

"I want to hear any answers you're willin' to give."

"Well, you've heard 'em. 'Fraid it's not gonna get any better. Let's leave it alone and go on in."

They danced the slow ones together over in the dark corner but when a swing dance number or a two-step was struck up he didn't know how and he stepped aside and Ramona danced it with whoever asked. He often slipped out to the truck for a nip while she danced. Ed didn't show, but Lulu Bell did and she'd join him in the truck and shared the pint he'd brought and they finished it before the dance was half over. It was good commercial whisky, but he missed the fiery snorts of Ed's corn brew.

Sometime after midnight they lay in his bed and talked long into the night, kept awake by late night coffee and pie Ramona had brought from the café. In the dark, snuggled up against the chilly spring night, he asked her why she came back when she could have gone anywhere.

"I think it was my marriage fallin' apart like it did. I grieved for the longest while and then one day it come to me that I was all worked up over somethin' that never was real in the first place. That's when I started sortin' out what in my life was real and what was made up. I made my marriage up the same way a storyteller makes up a tall tale. If you're not careful, you end up makin' up most things and missin' out on the real ones."

They lay a while and listened to spring peepers sing love songs.

"What mom and dad had seemed real enough," he said.

"What they had was real I imagine. I'm sayin' what was real between them had nothin' to do with standin' up in front of a preacher. Any couple can get married and most women set great store by it, some men too, but they're wrong. It's just words somebody made up a long time ago, pretty words, and that's all. There's nothin' wrong with it, it just don't mean much."

"What if a couple means it when they say their vows? Dudn't that make a difference?"

"They'd mean it anyway, even without the vows. A lot of real things go unsaid, and a lot of said things are unreal."

"You make that up yourself?"

"Just now, just for you. You should know. You and Janeen had a pretty good run. I don't know what happened at the end."

"I felt her slippin' away. I guess one day she crossed some line and then she was closer to Larry than she was to me. They'd worked together for years. I counted on her being my wife more than I should of."

"You can't count on those old labels. You never know when

they're goin' to fall off or when someone's gonna slap a new one on."

"Well it's a different way of lookin' at things than I'm used to. Anyway I'm not sure I can tell what's real and what's not. I thought there was somethin' real with Janeen. I found out better. Maybe it was real for me but not for her. I don't know. It makes my head hurt to think about it."

"Best not to then probly."

"Can't help it. It's a lot like the old war wound. You hurt in a place that isn't even a part of you anymore."

They lay very still, beginning to get sleepy.

"Since you're so smart, maybe you can tell me what to do about the fix I'm in."

"I can, but you won't do it."

"What?"

"I know you. It won't be manly enough."

"Tell me anyhow."

"Hunker down."

"That's not much of an answer. It don't solve nothin'."

"It could if you did it long enough and didn't care what folks thought."

"So you'd just recommend doin' nothin' is what you're sayin'."

"Yeah, basically. Sometimes doin' nothin' is harder than it sounds."

"I'm kind of expected to do somethin', ain't I?"

"Oh yeah. Everbody's just settin' back and waitin' to see what kind of show you'll put on. Gossipmongers are salivatin' for you to go off the deep end and do something completely crazy. They're cocksure you'll get pushed till you break."

"Maybe I'll make 'em happy. Still up in the air yet."

"It won't make me happy. I can tell you that."

"What would make ya happy? Ya figured out that one?"

"If you stayed around and out of trouble and we could find out if what we got is real or not. That'd be a good start."

Clay waited until his mother and step-dad left for work and then he got Lonnie's old Army duffel bag out of the closet and started packing. Janeen had offered him a ride to school, but he had told her he'd rather walk.

Culling through his clothes, he rejected nearly all of the nice newer outfits his mother had bought him over the past few months, opting instead for worn jeans, tees, white cotton socks, and blue work shirts. He did throw in the western shirt and new jeans his dad had brought. He went into the bathroom and gathered a few basic toiletries, toothbrush, deodorant, comb, shampoo, razor and a new bar of soap.

Before he left, he made his bed and straightened things up. He picked up a copy of *The Red Pony* and held it over the bedspread and riffled the pages. Greenbacks fluttered down and he picked them up and stacked them, folded them in two and stuck them in his pocket. By the front door, he leaned the duffel, and he went to the kitchen and made two sandwiches and wrapped them in wax paper. After zipping them into the bag, he threw it over his shoulder, took his hat off the rack and put it on and went out the door.

It was a good traveling day, warm and sunny with a flotilla of cotton-ball clouds drifting across. He walked the few blocks to Eleventh Street, the path Route 66 took through Tulsa, and he waited on the corner a few minutes and caught a city bus. He got off near the bridge over the Arkansas and walked to the east end and stuck out his thumb.

A few minutes later a westbound Chevy pick-up with two cowboys up front pulled over and the driver pointed to the back and he tossed in the duffel and climbed in. Bags of cattle feed filled most of the bed, but he moved a few around and make himself a nest out of the wind and leaned back and watched Tulsa recede into his past.

Sunday afternoon Lonnie and Ramona drove up to Leonard's house. He needed to tell him about the death of the cows and the legal impasse he faced which might keep him from selling the land to his old friend. It was a bright cheery day and the Cookson Hills were fresh and dark green and rolled like a washboard across the landscape as they drove north into the Cherokee Nation. Ramona's dark hair flowed in the air rushing into the truck cab and she looked like a Choctaw princess running in the wind. The old truck smoked along straining up hills, hurdling downhill and shuddering if he pushed it past sixty.

They stopped in Tahlequah for a burger then headed up highway ten and turned to the east near Sparrowhawk Mountain onto a pocked and rocky road that climbed up switchbacks and sent jolts through the frame of the pick-up. After several miles of twists and climbs through stunted hardwoods, he turned onto a narrow opening, hardly more than a wide trail and limbs brushed the sides of the truck as he drove up and down through unspoiled hollows finally splashing through a creek before heading up Leonard's hill. The house was small and square with a pyramidal tin roof and stood up well off the ground on stacks of flat rocks. Dogs and small children peeked out from underneath the house when they pulled up in the yard.

Leonard took the news stoically as if he halfway expected things to turn out that way. He showed more interest in Ramona, cutting glances at her more than once. Lonnie couldn't tell if Leonard approved or disapproved of his having a Choctaw girlfriend. Leonard's tiny Cherokee wife served them lunch, scrambled eggs with wild onions, roast pork, poke salad greens, hot fry bread served in a buck brush basket, and big glasses of iced tea. They were an odd looking couple, Leonard big and imposing but slow moving and gentle and she twittering about like a bird, energetic and thin. The five coppery children ate at two card tables Leonard set up on the porch.

After lunch, Leonard took them for a horseback ride over the old outlaw trails which wound through the hills and topped out at Goat's Bluff. Leonard owned only one saddle so Lonnie and Ramona rode bareback using rope hackamores instead of bridles. But it didn't matter because the old swayback horses they rode were slow and docile and needed little guidance from their riders following the trails from memories of many previous trips. They ascended rocky wooded slopes only to descend into the next hollow, the trails cutting diagonally up and down the slopes. It was cool under the canopy of leaves and the sun rarely reached their faces before they rode out on top of the bluff.

Goat's Bluff jutted four hundred feet above the surrounding terrain and the view from its limestone cap across the carpet of treetops was blurred by blue haze over the green-clad distant hills. They dismounted and rested, enjoying the sanctity of trees and rocks, and saying little to disturb the woodland spirits. Leaves rustled, squirrels barked, jays chattered and the horses clomped their hooves on the rocks and cropped grass during rest stops. On the ride back they stopped at a spring and watered the horses and got cool drinks from the crystalline pool below the seep. In the late afternoon, clouds scudded in and the sky began to darken and the first undulating rolls of thunder reached them as they arrived back at Leonard's house. Leonard and Lonnie put the horses up in the barn, which he noticed was in better shape than the house, and tended to their needs and then they sat in Leonard's small living room and drank coffee setting their cups on a table made from a cable spool.

Leonard tried to get them to stay to dinner, but they wouldn't, and Lonnie tried to get Leonard to take some money for the dead cows, but he wouldn't, so they drove off in the midst of a thunderstorm and headed home. The rain sizzled under the tires as they rocked along. Ramona leaned on his shoulder in the close atmosphere of the closed up cab and slept all the way to Sallisaw.

In the dream Janeen was pounding on his door calling out his name but he was paralyzed and unable to get up and respond. Her voice was beckoning him with a certain desperate quality he remembered from a past life. I should really go see why she's suddenly at my door. I once loved her, I still love her, I'll always love her. But he was immobilized, unable to act, even though he wanted to. She rattled the lock and he thought he heard a sob.

His eyes popped open. Startled and stiff, he realized Janeen really was calling his name and knocking loudly. He jumped into some jeans and pushed his hair back and wondered what the hell was going on. He jerked the door wide open and he and his ex stood face to face and there was an awkward moment when neither of them knew how to start. Despite being distraught, Janeen looked good in jeans and a fuzzy sweater. Morning light picked up red highlights in her chestnut hair. Larry sat out in a shiny Lincoln and stared up at the porch.

"Come on in."

"I'd rather not." Her face became more composed.

"I'm lookin' for Clay. He's run off and I thought he might have showed up here."

"Haven't seen him. You could of called and saved yourself a long drive."

"I did call until after midnight last night. I guess I know where you were."

He stood there silently, still not quite awake and at a disadvantage to duel with Janeen.

"Well, he ain't here. You and Larry drove a long way for nothin'."

"You better not be lyin' to me, Lonnie Stewart. I'll find out if you're hidin' him out here, if you're sneakin' around."

"You're a fine one to talk about sneakin' around."

"Oh, just go to hell. I shoulda known better than to expect a straight answer out of you."

She did an about face and stomped away toward the steps.

"I told ya he's not here. I ain't seen him nor heard from him."

She turned around at the top of the steps.

"Honestly? Lonnie, I'm worried sick."

"When did he turn up missin'?"

"He didn't come home from school yesterday. I thought he might have gone to a friend's house. He wasn't there and it turns out he never made it to school yesterday."

Lonnie felt a little queasy lump forming in his stomach.

"Have you called the cops?"

"Yeah, last night. They say he has to be missing twenty-four hours before they'll even take a missing person report. He's not in jail, that's all they could tell me. I'm goin crazy. I just knew he'd be here with you."

He didn't know what to say. He felt funny standing there barefoot and shirtless with sleep still in the corners of his eyes.

"You want some coffee?"

She looked at him wide-eyed, deliberating.

"I can't."

"Oh shit, it's only coffee. Get Larry in here and let's see what we can figure out."

It was not a scene he ever would even have imagined, the three of them sitting around his battered kitchen table having what amounted to a tea party. He got his shirt and shoes on and washed his face, but it was still more like a dream, a bad one that he would like to wake up from instead of into.

They cradled their mugs and occasionally he or Janeen would throw out a possibility. Larry had said hello, but that was it.

"Did you check the hospitals?"

"Last night. Nothing."

They blew into their cups and took cautionary sips.

"He been actin' different, strange?"

"Not that I can tell. He's a little tired of school but he always gets restless this time of year."

The dogs came up to the back door and peered in, sure they were missing something important.

"You look in his room for a note, any sign he packed up, anything?"

"His room was neat as a pin, like he just cleaned it up. That bothered me some. He'll usually leave a few things lying around."

Her voice wavered and her hand went over her mouth and she set her mug down a little too roughly and coffee slopped out on the table. The phone rang just then and it was Ramona and he said, "Could I call you back in a little while?"

It had never been quieter in his house than it was while they finished their coffee. Larry gave Janeen his handkerchief and she mopped up her face, but it was still puffy and red. Lonnie couldn't think of a thing to say.

Janeen rose and headed toward the front door, Larry got up and followed and Lonnie trailed behind. She stopped framed in the doorway.

"Tell me if you hear from him. Call me day or night. I'll let you know if I find out anything."

She moved on out on the porch and Larry took her place in the doorway. He looked directly at Lonnie for the first time.

"Just want you to know Lonnie that what my father's doing, I'm not any part of it. I tried to talk him into stopping it, but I don't think he's goin' to. He's a hard case." He didn't wait for Lonnie to answer, just wheeled around and walked.

In the Lincoln, they sat far apart the way married couples do, and Janeen put on some sunglasses and they drove off in a whirl of dust. Lonnie stood out and watched the car, lost in thought, until after it was out of sight.

A week later he opened his post office box and pulled out a batch of bills and circulars and there it was, a picture postcard, which read Denver, The Mile High City, and showed a big city skyline against a backdrop of snow-capped peaks. On the reverse side he recognized Clay's handwriting.

> *Hey Dad, I'm headed west. Just couldn't take it any more in Tulsa so I lit out and here I am. Don't worry about me. I've got enough money to last a while and I'll keep in touch Don't tell Mom where I am. She'd just try to drag me back. Love, Clay*

Two days later he pulled another card out of the box postmarked Colorado Springs.

> *Hey Dad, Denver is just too big a town so I bought a bus ticket and came down to Colorado Springs. I'm doing fine. How is everything down there? Good I hope. I'll keep in touch I promise. I'm wearing the jeans you gave me. No phony rules here. Love, Clay*

"What ya think they'll do?"
"Oh they'll shoot ya. They're a mean lot."
"Shoot me or kill me?"

"Depends on how much trouble you give 'em. They'd just about do one as the other. Buncha hired thugs."

"How 'bout you? Everything settled?"

"I'll go in in two weeks. Maybe we can share a cell."

"They're not takin' me off to jail."

"They're not takin' you off to jail." Disdain accented Ed's voice.

"I didn't do nothin'."

"Not yet you didn't. You're gonna have to do somethin' though when they show up at your door armed to the teeth."

They were about half drunk, working on the other half. Ed passed the bottle.

"Man has to make a stand sometime or he's just not a man."

"Guess that's right, but dying ain't much of a livin', son. You gotta think about who else is involved here."

"It's my fight. I'm not involvin' anyone else."

"Oh, I know how feisty and standoffish you are. You got marks all over you where people have been touching you with twenty-foot poles. But goddamn it Lonnie, if you go and get yourself killed while I'm in jail I'm gonna come walk all over your grave."

"You'd do that for me?"

"Shit, Lonnie, I ain't even first in line. There's Ramona, Clay, your sister, Homer, Janeen."

"Janeen, now you're reachin'."

"Maybe, I don't think so."

They sat a while and looked off into the distance where a hawk was making lazy circles on the thermals.

"What about Lenora?"

"Well, I guess she'd miss you in her own way."

"No, I mean what about when you go inside?"

"She'll manage. Probly think it's a vacation."

Ed took a long draw on the bottle then held it up to see how much was left and passed it to Lonnie.

"Finish it. Chug."

Lonnie chugged and then wiped his mouth with the back of his hand.

"You know what I'd do if I could?"

Ed just looked at him and waited.

"I'd make it a law that if you didn't make whisky, you get thown in jail."

"That'd take all the fun out of it. You know what I'd do?"

"No tellin'."

"I'd run for sheriff."

He tried to stop the days from slipping away by refusing to look at the drugstore calendar by the back door. He tried to follow old routines, to pretend that nothing was different. He rode out on old Buster almost every day, thinking this is all gonna be covered with water and people are going to be runnin' ski boats right through here. It seemed like an unreal idea. Old Buster seemed to enjoy the rides as much as he and often he would get down and walk a mile or two to limber up and give the old horse a break.

A week before he was supposed to lose title to the land, another card arrived from Clay, postmarked, Delta, Utah.

> *Hey Dad, I'm on my way to California on a Greyhound bus. I'm doing OK. Tomorrow I'll be looking at the ocean. Hope you are well. I'll write again soon. Love, Clay.*

He tried to keep busy. It was time for the first cutting so he called Homer and got him to bring his equipment over. Homer cut the lush growth bearding the low prairie hills for two days and by the time he was done the sun had dried the hay where he had started cutting enough to start baling. Homer cut and baled the hay on halves. Lonnie used his old truck to haul his half of the bales to the rickety old barn. He had to be careful. Copperheads crawled up under the hay bales and you might grab up a bale and heft it up only to find a snake thick as a chair leg hanging out of the bale and mad as hell at being disturbed.

When Homer finished baling he doubled back and helped Lonnie haul out bales to the barn and then they used both their trucks and hauled Homer's bales over to his place. By the end of the third day, as the sky turned cerise, the first cutting was in the barns and they celebrated with a trip to the café.

Ramona was her usual cheery self, but she looked a little tired and drawn and he wondered if the situation was wearing on her. But then she'd been serving tables all day so maybe she was just exhausted from being on her feet so long. It was close to closing time when she brought their orders, roast beef for Lonnie, fried chicken for Homer, and after she topped up their coffee cups she slid in beside Lonnie until their hips touched. Lonnie and Homer shoveled away at their portions.

"You boys worked up quite an appetite. Guess you did an honest day's work."

They both nodded, mouths full.

"Don't work too hard now Lonnie. I want you light on your feet for the dance Saturday night. You won't be able to keep up if you're wore out."

"Nobody could keep up with you anyway," Lonnie managed between bites.

Ramona jostled his elbow in response causing him to drop a bite of mashed potatoes onto the formica.

"I expect you boys will be wanting some pie. Tell me what kind you want and I'll go ahead and go get it."

He itched all over from the hay bits that had found their way into his clothing so he bathed as soon as he arrived home. While he was toweling off, the phone rang and it was Janeen. She told him she had gotten a postcard from Clay and she believed he was in Colorado Springs and she and Larry were going to drive there and try to find him.

He didn't say much, just thanked her for letting him know and got off the phone as soon as he could. He couldn't help feeling guilty knowing she was in for a long drive with no hope of finding Clay at the end of it. But he kept his own counsel and kept quiet about what he knew about Clay's whereabouts. If anything happened to Clay some of the responsibility would rest with him he knew, but since he was forced to divide his loyalties, he cast his lot with his son. Janeen would have his hide if she found out but he just hoped she wouldn't.

Another card came the next day. It showed the Golden Gate Bridge and sailboats skimming over dark blue water. The postmark read San Francisco.

> *Dear dad, I waded barefoot in the Pacific Ocean today. I was surprised it was so cold. I'm a little lonesome but pretty much OK and I still have plenty of money to live on. I'll keep in touch. Hope everything well at home. Love, Clay.*

Home, Clay had called it, his home. It made him feel a pang of hopefulness.

The letter lifted his spirits somehow. He got out and cleaned and oiled all the guns. He groomed old Buster till his coat was shiny and clean. The house needed a good cleaning and straightening up and he spent the afternoon sweeping, dusting, scrubbing, and polishing. For the first time in ages he washed the old truck and cleaned up the interior of the cab. He was rewarded. Far back under the seat he found a quart fruit jar of Ed's whisky which had been quietly aging for who knows how long. He took one long quaff to test the quality and then set it on the porch to help pass the evening.

Late in the day a pickup turned into the long drive and pulled up by the house. Sheriff Joe Johnson climbed out. He was a big athletic man, wearing a straw hat, jeans, cowboy boots and a khaki shirt with a dull silver star pinned to the pocket. He wore mirrored sunglasses and a large-caliber Colt revolver flapped against his hip as he walked across the yard. Lonnie had never met him but knew him by reputation, a tough man, a former professional boxer, and after that a rodeo bull rider. He enforced the law using the golden rule, those who have the gold rule, and he lived well, far above what his county salary of a few thousand dollars could possibly provide.

The sheriff didn't extend his hand and neither did Lonnie who sat on the porch steps and didn't get up.

"You're the Stewart boy, I take it."

"Could be."

"Lonnie, I thought I'd make a friendly visit out here. From what I hear you've been sayin' you're plannin' some kind of standoff or some such foolishness. That right?"

"Don't plan to do nothin' but live peaceful on family land. That's not agin' the laws these days is it?"

"No, but staying on another man's land is. Your place done sold and you been paid. I'll be comin' out here in a few days to enforce a court order and you'd best be shed of this place by then. It don't make no difference to me one way or t'other, but it could mean a big difference to you."

"Meanin' you're gonna shoot me?"

"If you resist I may have to. I hope it dudn't come to that, but if I have to it won't be the first time. Wouldn't bother me much neither."

"Sheriff, was you raised around here?"

"Shore was, family's been here since before statehood."

"If a man was to come out and tell you he was fixin' to run you off the old home place, how would you take it?"

"I didn't put my family land up for sale on the open market. If I had I'd expect to move over for the man that bought it. I reckon that's what you oughta do."

"Just roll over for Uncle Henry, huh? That's your advice?"

"From what I heard, you was wantin' to leave anyways."

"There's leavin' and there's getting' pushed out. When somebody pushes me I push back."

"I's told you was a hard man to reason with. Guess I heard right. You'd best start packin' up. That'd be the thing to do."

"Let me ask you one thing, sheriff. How's it feel to be a hired mouthpiece?"

The sheriff's lips hardened and thinned and he stood up a little straighter.

"I didn't have to come out here, ya know. This is a friendly visit. The next one won't be."

"Sheriff, you better get off my land."

"What's that?" the sheriff asked pointing at the quart jar of liquor beside Lonnie.

"What do you think it is?"

"I think it's contraband. Guess I'm gonna have to do my duty."

With a movement like a gunfighter, the sheriff pulled the big Colt out and cocked it all in one motion and stretched out his arm and fired. The fruit jar exploded in a spray of glass and moonshine. The blast echoed for a while and Lonnie's ears rang. A shard flew up and stuck just over his cheekbone and blood trickled down over his lip and onto his chin. A hole the size of an egg was left in the boards of the porch. Smoke curled from the barrel of the Colt.

The sheriff started to re-holster his piece but when Lonnie stood up he decided to keep it out and started walking sideways toward his truck never taking his eyes off Lonnie. Walking a few paces behind, Lonnie followed him across the yard shellshocked, a goofy grin cracking his face like the sheriff had just solved all his problems. When he reached the truck, the sheriff pointed the gun at Lonnie's chest as he reached for the door handle. Lonnie stopped and waited until the sheriff climbed in. Before the sheriff hit the starter he spoke.

"You be careful sheriff. And next time bring your water skis."

The sheriff gave him a dark and mystified look, like Lonnie was as crazy as he'd heard, and fired up the pickup and drove off in a swirl of dust.

After dark he sat out on the porch and watched mist submerge the meadow and turn blue under the rising moon. The dogs joined him on the porch and listened expectantly for his voice, but he could find no words for them. He drank bootlegged rum until he was loose and went and lay down and tried to sleep, but sleep would not settle on him He turned the pillow to the cool side every few minutes, and shifted and turned and finally drifted into a light doze as the moon slid downhill toward morning. His light sleep was broken when the dogs broke into a frenzied alarm in the pre-dawn murk. He rose quickly and grabbed a flashlight and slipped out into the yard and the cone of light captured a skunk waddling belligerently toward the weeds.

He gave up on sleep and put the coffee pot on and sat in a kitchen chair and sipped at the strong bitter brew while he waited for the sun to fade the eastern horizon. After his second cup, a gray light filtering over the edge of the world proclaimed the new day. He got in his old truck and drove to town. The café was open, a few early risers ensconced in their usual places. None of them seemed to note his arrival except for Ramona.

"What happened to your face?"

"Just a scratch."

She had no time to ask for details, just took his order and poured coffee and gave him a worried look.

His food came, scrambled eggs, sugar cured bacon, a big old biscuit and cream gravy with chunks of pork sausage.

"Awful busy to be so early."

"Game day's always a madhouse. You're up and around early."

"Thought I'd get a jump on the day for once."

"You goin' to the game?"

"Don't imagine I will"

"Your sister and nephew are goin' to disown you one of these days."

"Reckon they might." He looked down at the breakfast laid out in front of him.

"Well, I gotta work. Will I see you later?"

"Probly not."

He went back to the house and spent the morning gathering up things that were precious to him. A lock of his mother's hair, family photos, an old Barlow pocket knife his dad had given him, the family Bible with its recorded births, marriages, deaths, one of Janeen's old handkerchiefs, still faintly redolent of Blue Waltz, his high school letter, a tin horse he had scissored from a tobacco tin. All except the pocket knife he slipped into the pages of the Bible and he wrapped the Bible in a piece of oilcloth and tied a pigstring around it and put it in his old Army rucksack, tossing the knife in afterwards and setting the pack by the back door.

A fly was buzzing against the back screen, butting repeatedly into the wire, furious and confounded by the barrier. He watched the fly batter against the wire, bouncing back again and again until it was exhausted and then lighting on the doorframe to rest. He stood very still and watched the fly and he could see its sides heave in and out from the exertion. He knew what would happen, of course. The fly would eventually bang itself to death against the screen even though there was a crack the size of his little finger at the top of the sagging door and the fly could escape easily if it would only try to go around the obstacle it was facing. Feeling magnanimous he pushed the door open and it flew out and several others flew in.

He straddled a kitchen chair backwards and sat listening to the day. A mourning dove was calling plaintively, sounding like someone blowing across the lip of a bottle. A dry scouring wind had whistled up strong enough to rattle the loose tin on the roof and the dogs were restless, pads softly thumping the porch boards. The groan of a truck in low gear reached him and he stood up and looked out to see Ed's truck kicking up a roostertail of dust on the river road.

Ed had started drinking early and was in a jovial red-faced haze of inebriation.

"Buy a condemned man lunch," he proposed.

Lonnie assented and they climbed in Ed's truck and drove to the café. It was early for lunch and the café was quiet. The old cook came out of the kitchen with a pen and pad in his hands and came over to take their order.

"Where's Ramona?"

"She ran home for a while. She'll be back."

They ordered hot roast beef sandwiches with mashed potatoes and brown gravy and coleslaw and glasses of iced tea. It was the lunch special. The cook went back and after a couple of minutes of clattering plates emerged with heaping portions and slid the lunches in front of them and set out their drinks in tall glasses.

Lonnie and Ed wolfed the food, Ed grinning between bites like it was a pie-eating contest and Lonnie subdued and contemplative. A few more midday diners filtered in and plopped onto the oilcloth seats of the booths near the window. The cook came back out and asked if they wanted dessert. They declined. Lonnie found himself looking through the plate glass for Ramona's familiar form.

She still hadn't shown by the time they had finished the meal, two cups of coffee and two cigs each. The café was filling with hungry people and the old cook was running frantically between the kitchen and the tables trying to keep up. A puzzled Lonnie paid and they walked out and got in Ed's truck and as he started it up. Just then Ramona and the young rancher pulled up in front of the café, talking and laughing, and she kissed him goodbye passionately before she got out and hurried into the café.

Ed gave Lonnie a look like, "What the hell was that?" and backed out and roared off down the main drag. The meat, potatoes and coleslaw lay heavy in Lonnie's stomach and he kept swallowing because his throat felt constricted. He was breathing shallowly and rapidly and finally he just closed his eyes and leaned back in the passenger seat and flipped out the wing window so the air would flow over him. He felt like a sinking rock thrown into the river.

"Sum bitch, sum bitch," Ed kept saying under his breath.

When they got back to Lonnie's place some serious drinking started. Ed dug out a quart of Johnny Walker Black he'd been saving for a special occasion, although his original thought had been that it would be used to reinforce some happy event but he was just as willing to let it anesthetize an unhappy one. So they sat cross-legged on the worn pine boards of the living room floor and passed the fat bottle back and forth pouring down long glugs, their Adam's apples bobbing like fishing corks in a river of whisky.

When the bottle was at about half-mast, Ed noticed the cleaned and oiled firearms resting against the wall.

"How bout a little target practice?" It was the first thing either of them had said since town. Lonnie looked up grimly.

"Might's well. May be doin' some serious shooting real soon, seems like."

They stuffed their pockets with all calibers of cartridges and carried the guns and the bottle out into the oblique hard afternoon light. They leaned the rifles against a barbed wire fence and Ed walked off fifty lanky paces and set the bottle on the ground at that point. The rules were simple. If you hit, it was your option to take a slug of whiskey or not. If you missed, you tipped the bottle back and took a big swallow.

They started out with the old peacemaker, setting tin cans on top of a fencepost and blasting away. The heavy old Colt was not easy to shoot, hard to hold steady, requiring two hands in the billowing winds, and kicking up forcefully when its heavy loads exploded under the hammer.

"Could you tell where that one went?"

"I think you were high right."

"How can you tell?"

"Can't, just know that old piece kicks that way usually."

Ed took a shot out of the bottle and set it down to mark the toeline.

Lonnie stared hard down the barrel for long moments and blew a chunk out of the side of the post six inches below the can, which wobbled and fell off.

"That don't count."

"I know it don't."

Lonnie took the required dose and went and reset the target for Ed.

They both blasted away again without results and then again and the can still stood proudly atop the post. Lonnie reloaded and Ed took dead aim and the can flew away into the pasture.

"Good shot."

"Got lucky."

Lonnie set up a new can and they went through the second round of cartridges with the target unscathed but the whiskey was percolating into their veins and their nerves were leveling out and on the second reload they both blew away cans.

"I'm ahead two to one," Ed said.

"Just got 'nuf shells left to reload once."

"Aim careful."

Ed killed one can, Lonnie two and it was tied three-three and they were out of ammo for the Colt.

"Let's try the saddle gun," Lonnie said, sliding 30-30 cartridges in and levering one home. They both picked off cans perfectly shot after shot and the remaining whiskey set untouched.

"This is too easy, like shootin' the broad side of a barn," Ed complained.

"Load up the twenty-two," Lonnie said.

Lonnie pulled a kitchen match out of his pocket and stuck it in a crack in the fence post.

"See ya hit that, hot shot."

Ed grinned and bore down and blew the matchstick in two on the first shot and then Lonnie steadied the long barrel of the twenty-two and did the same. Lonnie had a full box of fifty brass jacketed twenty-twos and in the late day light they glowed golden as he slipped them into the magazine seventeen at a time. The two of them splintered matches on about half the shots and the whiskey rolled easy down their throats when they missed. The rifle felt natural like an extension of Lonnie's arm and when he missed it was nearly always when his mind drifted off to Ramona.

"Dead-eye shootin'," Ed said and blew another matchstick to pieces. "Wanna raise the ante?"

"Name your poison."

"First one to strike the match, other one chugs."

Lonnie whistled a long descending note and picked up the twenty-two.

The light was fading as they shot round after round trying to graze the match head into flame. They blew more matches apart, knocked the head off, sent bullets wide, high and low, reloaded two more magazines, squinted hard in eagle-eyed concentration, embraced the rifle like it was flesh and blood, relaxed their trigger pull till the curved metal moved only imperceptibly, and then finally, as the light waned, Ed brushed the match just right and it burst into flame. Lonnie picked up the bottle, tipped it high and drained the last four fingers of amber elixir and tossed the bottle into the weeds.

"Stick with me bud and I'll learn ya how to shoot."

"Hell, I just wanted the last of the whiskey. Thought you'd never get around to lightin' up that match. Got any more?"

They lay out by the pasture and drank Ed's emergency bottle he kept stashed under the spare tire and watched the stars emerge in a sky the color of new blue jeans.

"Wanna talk about it?" Ed ventured.

"Naw, don't wanna talk, don't wanna think, don't wanna do nothin'."

"Ya never can know 'bout them things."

"Well, it ain't like she was wearing my class ring around her neck or nothin'."

"You know what I'd do if I could?"

"No tellin' but I bet I'll find out."

"I'd run away from Lenora just as hard and fast as I could."

"What's stoppin' ya?"

"Well, I reckon it's mostly seein' how you moped around this last year since Janeen took off. I used to think I'd get enough and up and leave her one day but not no more."

"And all this time I thought you was a good family man."

"I am, old son, I am, but not by choice."

"Well, most of the time, the choices are made for ya. They're made by your wife, your kids, your boss, the goverment, the preachers, the bankers, the schools, the cops. Even the weather is decided for ya. When it comes right down to it, you don't call nary many shots and most of them is pissant stuff like what socks you put on that day or whether you have fries with that burger or whether you part your hair on the left or right and you know none of that shit really matters anyway."

"So what's a man to do?"

"Drift, Ed, just drift along. No need tryin' to fight it."

"This from a bullhead like you? The man who was stayin' around mainly because they was tryin' to make him leave?"

"Yeah, well, I'm tired and drunk and disappointed with life in general. Screw it all Ed. That's my new philosophy. You know you and I could just up and take off together and see where the road takes us. Could be a big adventure, see the country, bum around a while. As of today I've got one less reason to stay around and you've got enough hangin' over your head to run away from. How bout it old pal?"

"Is that you or the whiskey talkin', bud?"

"Little of both I imagine."

It got dark and the cool crept in and it felt just right and the stars twirled around some and Lonnie felt limp and the grass was soft against his back. They lay there in a comfortable silence listening to a nighthawk call and then Lonnie fell into a deep oblivious slumber.

He woke up damp with dew and the strangeness of wondering for a moment why he was not in his bed. Then a flickering light struck his eyelids and he heard a crackling noise and there was yellow light playing across the grass and he sat up so fast it made his head swim and his eyes lit up with the house ablaze. His first instinct was to look around for Ed but he was long gone and his second thought was to grab a gun and he crawled around in the wet grass looking for a weapon until he came across the 30-30 saddle gun but it was empty as was the Colt revolver and when he found it, so was the twenty-two. He went into his pockets and on the ground for cartridges but found none.

So he stuck the Colt in his waistband, picked up the rifles, stood up and made a dash for the house and before he reached the back door a rifle cracked and he heard a bee-like buzz and a bullet fly close by. He dived into the kitchen thinking he could maybe fight the fire but the house was filled with smoke and he began coughing and his eyes burned and closed involuntarily and he found himself lying helpless on his kitchen floor with the house burning down around him.

He crawled toward the back door and came across the knapsack and he grabbed it by the strap and lay on his belly by the back door as far from the fire as he could scoot. He eased the back door open just a crack and watched the yard as best he could with the fumes burning his eyes and steam rising from his wet clothes as the fire roasted him. The fire lit up the yard in uneven flashes and a light wind blew a cloud of smoke toward the barn. He heard the ceiling collapse in the living room and the flames heightened and licked all around him hungry to consume the rest of the house and he felt his skin beginning to blister and he felt his clothes might combust at any moment. He had no choice but to get out.

He worked his arms into the knapsack straps, picked up the rifles and bolted out the door and ran into the cover of the smoke, running low and hard all the way to the barn and he expected to be shot at any moment and the ground seemed to stretch out endlessly as he ran and he felt like a tin duck in a shooting gallery at the county fair but the smoke was thick and it was still dark out and he made it to the barn and shut the door behind him. Once inside he heard Old Buster nickering apprehensively, smelling the smoke. He threw down the knapsack and the useless guns and then climbed into the barn loft and from a loft window he watched his house burn to the ground.

He stayed in the barn until well after sunup and the daylight brought more revelations, the dogs poisoned and lying dead in a group, the tires of his truck slashed. The morning light also revealed that he was once again alone and the arsonists had slipped away under cover of darkness without his so much as laying eyes on one of them.

Ramona huddled in the dark little cafe bathroom off the kitchen sobbing hard. The news on everyone's lips that morning was that Lonnie's house burned to the ground during the night with him in it. The cafe buzzed like a beehive. It hit her like a punch in the stomach. A volunteer fireman told her only smoking embers remained and that it was impossible anyone could have survived. Lonnie's old truck still set out front.

The old cook had related how the afternoon before Lonnie had waited around for her and finally given up and left. At the time, it didn't seem like an important piece of information. Now it broke her heart.

A new wave of sobs rolled through her chest. She dabbed at her eyes and cheeks with toilet paper and blew her nose. Staring herself down in the mirror, she saw a woman hurtling into middle age with a puffy face and red eyes.

A light knock came on the door and the old cook said softly, "Ramona, you all right?"

She struggled for composure and managed to squeak out, "I'll be there in a minute." His old-man shuffle moved away from the door. She turned on the cold tap and splashed water on her face, dried off and quickly reapplied her make-up.

When she came out several orders were lined up waiting. She grabbed up the young rancher's order and carried it to his table and put the plates in front of him. He looked up at her with eyes filled with promise and expectation. She looked away and hurried back for the other breakfast orders.

As she hustled around among the regulars trying to catch up, many eyes fell on her, and the diners stopped talking when she came up to their table. When they met her gaze, it was sometimes with smug glances, derision, curiosity. She slopped coffee in their cups, clunked plates onto the oilcloth, and waited in the kitchen for them to leave without so much as a refill.

When the breakfast rush began to wane, she went out to bus the tables, and the sheriff and Henry Looper walked in talking and laughing. A dam inside her broke and before they could slide into a booth she screamed at them so loud and piercingly it hurt her throat.

"I'm not serving you sumbitches." Then she took off her apron, threw it on the floor and walked out.

By mid-morning Lonnie had buried the dogs behind the barn and had made up his mind what to do. He went in the barn and brushed old Buster till his coat gleamed chestnut highlights and then he saddled him up. He gathered up a few tools and the extra horse blanket and stuffed it all in the saddlebags. The 30-30 he slid into its scabbard and he tied the twenty-two across the pommel and hung the knapsack off the saddle horn. Then he swung up into the saddle and rode away from the smoldering ashes that had been his home and his life not looking back and grim-faced with determination he rode off down the road toward town. An hour later he was at the lawyer's office where he picked up the check for five thousand dollars and he walked across the street to the bank and the teller counted out fifty one hundred dollar bills into his hand. The next stop was Redwine's where he bought a few cans of beans, a hunk of bacon, coffee, three boxes of cartridges and a small skillet. He walked back over to where Buster was tied up in the alley behind the lawyer's office, loaded up the supplies and mounted up and rode out of town. As he passed behind the café his head turned that way in spite of himself and he caught a glimpse of Ramona carrying an armful of plates out of the kitchen. A pang went through him then but he turned back resolutely and looked down at the ground until he reached the edge of town.

It was of those glorious late summer days, the air cool and dry and the sky an intense blue with high cirrus feathering the domed firmament. Colorado weather. But he hardly noticed as old Buster walked steadily down dirt roads and out into the countryside. He stopped at a spring near old Fort Coffee and watered the horse and himself and let Buster crop grass for a few minutes. Then he rode on crisscrossing the county on back roads. Cars and trucks whizzed by and the drivers raised their hands in greeting and he nodded back like he was just out for a ride on a beautiful day. Old Buster seemed happy to be out for a walk and forged ahead at a good pace for a horse of his years.

He made another rest stop under a big oak at the side of the road and while Buster grazed he loaded up the 30-30 and slipped five fat cartridges into the Colt, leaving the chamber under the hammer empty. Then he rode on into the afternoon down more dirt roads taking a circuitous route through the rich bottomlands of the Poteau River until his uncle's big house heaved into view in the distance. He rode boldly up and tethered Buster to the gatepost. His uncle's big sedan was gone. Just for good measure he stuck the Colt under his belt. The front door was unlocked and he turned the knob and walked right in.

It had been many years since he had seen the inside of the house and he was surprised at how little things had changed. It had the same musty smell he remembered from his childhood and his grandmother's old flowered sofa still sat in the living room in the exact same spot he remembered. He walked through the rooms one by one making sure he was alone in the house and then he returned to the front room and sat down at his uncle's big mahogany desk against the inside wall.

He went into the desk drawers and started pulling out papers and stacking them on top of the desk, passbook savings accounts, old photos, deeds and abstracts, car titles, records of livestock transactions, feed bills, insurance policies, checkbooks, ledgers, all the accumulated paperwork. Crumbling the papers into rough balls, he made a mound on top of the desk. Then he picked up grandma's ornate coal oil lamp, unscrewed the top, and poured kerosene onto the papers. He pulled a kitchen match out of his pocket and struck it on his thumbnail and held it a moment cupping a hand around it watching it flame up and then he touched it to the soaked papers and they caught readily and yellow flames roared into life and black smoke began to belch up from the pile. Eyes starting to smart from the smoke, he stepped back a few paces and watched long enough to see the fire start crawling up the wall and then he turned and calmly walked out the front door leaving it open to feed the inferno with plenty of oxygen. He unhitched Buster, sprang into the saddle and turned the old horse, resisting looking back as he trotted into the cover of the trees.

Sheriff Joe Johnson was furiously organizing a posse to go after Stewart when the phone on his desk rang. He knew who it was, and what he was going to say, but he answered anyway.

"You better get him this time."

"I aim to. I'm handlin' it myself. I got fifty men under my command who know every inch of the ground he's runnin' on. I'm bringin' in hounds. Roadblocks on every highway. The National Guard is sending a helicopter. He dudn't have a chance."

"That's pretty much what you said the last two times."

"He's a wily one. I'll give you that. But he's shit out of luck this time. I'll track him into hell if I have to."

"You ever play baseball?"

Johnson looked perplexed and thought about his answer.

"Yeah, second base, and I batted clean-up."

"I guess you'll understand then when I say three strikes and you're out."

Johnson clenched the handset, his fingers turning white.

"I got my eye on the ball. Ain't no pinch hitter this time. Stewart is goin' down. He can't run fast enough or far enough to get away from me. This time tomorrow I expect to have him in custody or in the morgue."

"Dead or alive, but you could save the county the expense of a trial if it was dead. You get a shot, you take it. You do know how to shoot, don't ya?"

The sheriff looked at a 30.06 in the rack on his office wall.

"Wouldn't be surprised if it turned out that way. I doubt he'll go peaceable."

"I might be able to help you out a little."

"Come on out. Bring your horse. I can use ever man I can get."

"Not that way. I'm too old for that shit. But I can narrow the search. He's headed north. You'll pick up his trail headed in that direction."

"Somebody report a sighting to you?"

"Never mind how I know. I just do. Take it as gospel."

Johnson's mind flashed on the rumors he'd heard over the years of the little men who advised Looper. If that old bird didn't have so much money and pull, he'd just be another crazy old geezer. Still, without knowing where he got it, the information made sense. He'd already decided to head north with the posse right off.

"I'll start the search in that quadrant. It figures he's headed for the hills."

"You'll start it there, keep it there and finish it there. Your job depends on it. That clear enough?"

"I figured that's how it was. That's why I'm bringin' him in come hell or high water. I don't, I'll hand over my star."

"I'm gonna offer a reward. A thousand to the man who gets him. You tell your men."

"For a thousand, they'd go after the devil hisself. I'll tell 'em."

"You best stop gabbin' and get after it. Burnin' daylight."

The phone clicked and went dead. Johnson looked at the receiver for a few seconds and shook his head. Then he went back to calling up every man he knew who could sit astride an horse.

Later that day, Johnson rode uphill through the brush along the breaks north of the Arkansas River. Cresting a ridge, he sat his horse, pulled out a pair of binoculars and swept the scrub timber on the rolling promontories in front of him. A string of riders, each separated by about a hundred feet, moved methodically through the undergrowth along a mile-wide swath. The dogs had picked up Stewart's scent on the south bank of the river, but had been unable to find where he came out on the north side. He'd probably ridden through the shallows for a while in one direction or the other before crossing, the sheriff figured. If he were smart, and it looked like this one was, he came onto the north bank on rocky ground and left no tracks. But he couldn't be far ahead, probably no more than an hour or two. The net was closing.

The helicopter made a pass over the hills in advance of the line, the peculiar choppy pulse of the rotor reaching his ears. He kicked the flanks and his horse trotted down the hill to catch up with the line of mounted men.

They still had a few hours of light left, and Johnson thought his quarry would probably stop late in the day to make camp. Under the cover of twilight, they would close in on him, surround his bivouac, and there would be no chance of escape.

At the top of the next rise, he paused and pulled out his canteen and took a drink. In the near distance, the surface of Brushy Lake glimmered like a mirror. The lake would be a likely place to pitch a camp. He urged his horse down the hill, certain the chase was drawing to a close. After a long day on the trail, he could tell his mount was tiring and when his pace slackened, he kept the horse at a brisk walk with his rowels. The word was that Stewart was riding an old horse and that was another reason he was confident they would catch up to him.

At the bottom of the hollow the trail leveled out and ran straight under blackjack and post oak, the ground covered with coral berry, blackberry briars and sumac. His horse put his head down and labored up the next rocky hill, following a sinuous game trail. In the deep afternoon shade, neither horse nor rider saw the big rattlesnake in their path until they were almost upon it and when the horse's hoof dislodged a stone and it struck the snake, the rattler coiled and whirred and hissed.

Taken by surprise, the horse panicked and reared on the upslope. Johnson made a grab for the saddle horn and missed and fell out of the saddle and hung by a foot stuck in the right stirrup. He dangled there for a long moment while the horse teetered and wobbled and tried to get his balance on the unlevel ground. Then the horse fell over backwards, pulled over to one side by Johnson's bulk, and fell on top of him, and a thousand pounds of falling bone and muscle crushed him into the earth.

Nostrils flared, the horse scrambled up and took off downhill at a gallop, dragging Johnson's broken body. The rattler gave a last warning hiss and slithered off into the leaf litter.

Part IV

Flight

Lonnie sat out on the porch sharpening the stub of a pencil, drinking coffee and surveying the new day. It was early October and spring was greening the pampas turning the tableland into rich pasture for the horses grazing out in the fields around the little cabin. He was whittling away at the pencil in preparation for writing a few letters to people in his old world, and he was thinking about what he would say to each of them. It was a breathless morning, so still and quiet that he could hear the horses snorting and chomping at the new grass from where they grazed far out on the flats and the silence was so perfect that when a vee of black-necked swans flew over, the beating of their wings was audible and he looked up and watched their graceful flight toward a nearby *laguna*.

Fernando appeared around the corner bringing him his usual breakfast, *bife a caballo*, a thick steak topped with a fried egg. The old man was a good cook and Lonnie knew the steak had been grilled skillfully over a bed of coals and would be tender and juicy just as it had been for the two months since the old gaucho had taken over all the cooking duties. Plate in hand with the delicious aroma of broiled beef wafting up at him, Lonnie put aside the pencil and his thoughts of his former life and concentrated on enjoying his breakfast and the start of another day on the estancia.

A couple of minutes later Fernando joined him on the porch with his own steak and egg and a gourd full of *mate*. He eased himself down and sat cross-legged on the porch eschewing, as he always did, the use of a chair. Lonnie used the knife he had been using on the pencil to slice off strips of beef and impale them and lift them to his mouth. The old gaucho ate with gusto pulling from his wide belt a big knife, a *facon*, his most prized possession after his horse. He finished his food first and then waited until Lonnie had cleaned his plate and then took the dirty dishes around back to wash them up.

Lonnie had put off writing the letters for some time, choosing to immerse himself in the daily activities of getting his spread up and running. But his guilt had caught up with him finally and because he was planning to make the ride into the nearest town of any size the next day and he would have a chance to post mail, he had set himself a deadline and was resigned to writing to a few people back home before the day was out.

He got up and went inside to rummage around for his writing tablet. The cabin was just one big room, the kitchen in a leanto at the back, a sitting room at one end and his bed at the other. It was cozy, bright and new and the local workers had put it up in a matter of days, hauling out wagons of lumber from the nearest railhead and doing everything by hand right down to hewing out the window frames. It had a tin roof and a covered front porch and already in the weeks he had dwelt there, it had begun to feel like home. There was no electricity or running water, but somehow it pleased him with its simplicity and economy of design. He had it all to himself, Fernando preferring to live outside as he had done all his life.

He found the tablet and took it out to the porch. Fernando had saddled up his pony and was out doing his morning check of the remuda riding around in the peculiar one-hand style that all the gauchos used. He knew Fernando would tend to the horses well, looking over the brood mares to see that none were sick and tending to any cuts or scratches in his patient methodical way. He would make sure the Arabian blood stallion was not leading them too far away and herd them back in the direction of the cabin if they strayed too far afield. Fernando had a love for horses that rivaled his own passion and though they were separated somewhat by the barrier of language, the two of them had bonded strongly as soon as each of them discovered their mutual equine affections.

Fernando had been there when Lonnie arrived and purchased the land, as much a part of the landscape as the foxes and big hares who inhabited the place. It was Lonnie's guess that the old man had lived there most of his life, comfortable with only the sky for a roof and the flat earth for a bed, living off the land in a solitary existence. The two of them had come together as naturally as two men from such divergent places could, feeling each other out for a while, getting to know each other. Once they came to trust one another, an easy companionship had quickly developed and the two of them ran the place with no need for the unknown words of the other's language which both of them lacked.

The pampas was all open range and fences were rare, the land pristine, largely unspoiled by the hand of man. Often they would see gauchos from one of the nearby huge *estancias* riding across the land looking for maverick cattle and herding them back onto their home range. The big cattle ranches were a convenient source of fresh meat and the steaks they had eaten just that morning had been bought the day before at one of the bordering ranches which encompassed thousands of acres. His spread was small by comparison, a few hundred acres, though the local ranchers preferred the unit of hectares which he had learned equalled about two and a half acres.

He took a long last look out across the vast expanse to where the horizon lay, straight and uninterrupted as a still ocean, the sky bigger than any place he had ever seen, and then he licked the pencil lead and leaned his chair back against the wall and began to write.

> *Hey old boy,*
>
> *Just wanted to let you know that I'm alive and well and working hard getting a horse ranch going here in Argentina. You wouldn't believe how cheap land is here but everything costs a lot less here and a man can live on very little. The land is some of the richest I've seen and grows grass so thick the livestock can't keep it eat down. It's as good as any bottomland and flat as a pancake. You can ride a hundred miles in any direction without seeing so much as a slope. I bought almost 200 acres and had money left to buy horses. Right now I've got about 30 healthy young brood mares and a stallion with good blood lines. I've got an old gaucho helping out around the place and he is probably the best horseman I've ever seen. He has been trying to teach me some Spanish and I'm slowly beginning to talk the lingo. The weather here is different. First of all the seasons are all turned around backwards. While you're having fall we're just beginning our spring. Christmas will be in the middle of the summer. I got here in the winter and it was mild but I've heard the summers can be hot but I can't think they'll*

be any worse than Oklahoma. Did you work out your little problem? What's been happening around the old hometown? Do you miss your old drinking buddy? It got a little crazy after that night we had the shooting match, but I guess you heard by now. Don't know when I'll be able to come back, maybe never after what happened. Don't know if I want to anyway. I'm happier here than I've been in a while and I think I might just make a go of the horse ranch. Horses are still used a lot down here so there's a ready demand for them. Maybe it's the weather here but my leg doesn't bother me near as much anymore. Say hello to Lenora and the kids for me. I'd appreciate it if you'd keep my new address to yourself for reasons I know you understand. Drop by anytime.

Your old bud,
Lonnie

Fernando had ridden out until he was just a tiny silhouette against a plane of green. Lonnie knew he would stay out on horseback until time to begin preparations for the midday meal, *el almuerzo*. In fact, Fernando spent much of every day on horseback. Not that there was enough work to do to fill those hours. It was just that Fernando sat a horse the way most people sat a chair. He lived in the saddle.

He spent his days out there mingling among the herd of horses, and he knew each horse and each horse knew him. And the horses treated him as an equal, as one of them. If he called them, they came, if he spoke to them they listened and seemed to understand. Even the stallion deferred to him, seeing him as a partner and friend. Lonnie was convinced that if Fernando could have eaten and digested grass, the old gaucho could have lived among them as a member of the tribe and, if that was possible, it probably would have been his choice to do so.

A warm westerly wind, the *zonda*, made sitting out on the porch pleasant. Lonnie folded up the letter to Ed, sealed it in the envelope, and addressed it. He took out his dad's old Barlow knife and resharpened the pencil before he began writing the next letter.

Dear son,
   I once wanted to run off to California and swim in the ocean. Hope you are well and happy. I don't reckon you'd be able to guess where your old dad has up and gotten himself off to. I'm living the life of an Argentine rancher. I have a little spread and a herd of horses and an old gaucho who helps out and I guess he is about as close to a real cowboy as I will ever know. Don't know if you've been in touch with your mother or heard about my lighting out on my own. Hope I have not caused you any worry these last few months. Sometimes things happen that you never planned on and you go off in directions you did not expect. But I guess you already know that because you ran off even before I did. Blood will tell I guess. I miss getting to see you and I hope that sooner or later you will be able to come here and visit. It's a hell of a place and I think you would have the time of your life. I guess I've wanted to come down here ever since I heard about Will Rogers doing his cowpunching down here. It's like setting your watch back about a hundred years or so. There are more horses than cars and more open spaces than anything else. Even the stars at night are different here. Please write and let me know how you are doing. How is your mother, if you know? I guess you will not get to inherit the old family place like we planned. I guess this is sort of a secret but I found out they are going to put in a big lake and a lot of our land is going to be underwater when they get finished. But you might inherit a fine little horse

estancia down here instead. I'll be thinking of you. Let me hear from you.

Love,
Dad

The wind had picked up and ruffled the pages of his tablet. He felt a little stiff from inactivity so he got up and walked around a little and saw the water trough was low so he filled it up by hauling out fresh buckets of water from the hand dug well he and Fernando had labored so hard to dig beside the house. He looked around for something else to do but Fernando had taken care of everything and he had to go back to the porch and force himself to compose another letter.

> Dear Leonard,
>   Just wanted to write and thank you for all the help you gave me when I really needed it and to let you know I've turned up safe after a long trip south. I got my own place now and a good stock of breeding horses and I wish you were here with me because I know you would like it here. Say hello to old Buster for me the next chance you get and I hope he is happy there with you and your old horses. I hope you find that he is still a good mount and you will take him out on some rides because he would enjoy that. One of my few regrets is that I was not able to take him with me. Maybe I'll get back one of these days and pay you all a visit but don't look for me until you see me coming. Well, I guess they plan to dam up the river and flood the old homeplace. At least that is what I heard. What has been happening in Cherokee country? I wish I could sit down tonight to some good cooking like you get to eat all the time. Would you believe it is possible to get tired of eating steak? I'm sticking in a hundred dollars to

buy feed for old Buster and I hope it gets through to you alright. Say hello to everbody for me.

Your friend,
Lonnie

He only had one letter left to write so he stopped and rested a while and watched Fernando practice some of his gaucho tricks. When he had first seen the old man perform his routines, he was surprised at how spry he was. Some of the tricks required a helper and he was always willing to lend a hand just to see the show Fernando put on. The best known skill was throwing the *bolas*, three stones tied at the end of thongs and they were used primarly for hunting and a gaucho could throw them accurately in much the way American cowboys threw a lasso.

Lonnie had known of the *bolas* before he came south, but the other things Fernando could do came as a surprise. As he watched Fernando was practicing the *sortija*, riding at full tilt with a lance and picking off tiny dangling rings. The old man always reminded him of a medieval knight when he jousted at the rings. Another skill of timing and daring was called the *maroma* and it required a man to jump from the top of the corral fence onto the back of a running horse as it passed by. The gauchos used this skill as a way to mount rank wild horses they were breaking and Fernando was uncanny in his ability to made the leap and land astride the horse. Another trick, the one that required Lonnie's assistance was called the *pialar*. Fernando would gallop his horse at full speed past him while Lonnie twirled a lasso and tried to rope the horse's feet as it ran by. When Lonnie cast his rope successfully, the horse tripped and went tumbling. The trick was to leap from the horse's back and land on your feet on the ground with the reins in your hand. Gauchos sometimes encountered this kind of fall when their horses stepped into an animal burrow on the pampas.

Lonnie had to force himself to stop watching the old gaucho practice and return to scratching words across the page.

Dear Cousin Homer,

I guess you think I stole your horse and left you high and dry. You should feel better after you find the two hundred dollar bills I am enclosing and which I hope will make it back all the way to you without being stolen on the way. Let me know if you don't get them along with this letter. I made a mistake in ever selling you old Buster in the first place. I should of known better. Well, old couz, I think I've found the perfect place for a horseman like you or me. It's way down here in South America where horses are still important to folks and not just for pleasure rides. In fact the horses are the lifeblood of this place and without them I don't think you could run a cattle ranch and do any good. And cowboys, let me tell you these old boys down here can rodeo with the best. I've got an old cowhand living here who must be 30 years older than me and he can still outride, outrope and outlast me any day of the week. I'm living the life you and I used to talk about, raising horses on a nice little piece of flat prairie. I wish you could see my feisty little group of brood mares. I'm really looking forward to seeing the colts they will bear with my blood stallion. I remember you talking about the good bloodlines that came from Spain and you would be able to see in a second the pure blood in my Arabian sire. You can write me at the return address on the envelope and I sure hope you do. Keep my location a secret if you would because as I'm sure you know I've become something of an outcast in the old stomping grounds. Bet a long shot for me next time you go to the track. Take care now.

Your couz,
Lonnie

He mailed the three letters at the nearest town the next day and felt relieved to have an unwelcome chore finished. He had considered writing to Ramona and had actually gotten as far at the salutation, *Dear Ramona*, but words refused to flow out of him onto the page so he had eventually given up and abandoned the letter. Ramona had found what she wanted, he believed, a man willing to put down roots where he was planted, and he hoped she was happy. He saw no reason to revisit the past with her.

He was focused instead on the future. In the next few weeks Fernando and he built a barn, erected a windmill to pump water, and shopped around the neighboring countryside for more good mares to add to the brood. Lonnie bought a wagon and two sturdy draft horses to haul supplies from town. It was a funny looking rig to his eyes, more like a cart than a buckboard, the front wheels much smaller than the back wheels as if it were constantly rolling downhill. His Spanish improved to the point that he could use simple phrases and understand most of what was said to him, though he still thought in English and translated the words back and forth.

Time flowed by the way it will when your days are filled with passion for what you are accomplishing and once again it was time to make the trip to town to replenish the larder. The highlight of each trip was going to the *pulperia*, a combination general store, bar and bank. On this trip a red and white flag flew outside the building. Lonnie had learned that the white flag meant that tobacco, *hierba mate* and alcoholic drinks were available and the red flag signaled that fresh meat was in stock. He went inside and placed an order, which included all of the things the flags promised. In Argentina, he had come to accept that most all business matters required a wait so while his wagon was loaded with goods, he sat inside and sipped *clerico* at a small round table reading the letter which had arrived.

Lonnie, you old dog.

Up to now you could of been alive or dead for all I know. Lenora brought your letter up here yesterday. I'm the guest of the fedral govermint in Fort Smith but I may get out in just a few weeks if I can behave myself. Never mind my old hide. You pulled off a real doozie. Folks have been yapping their heads off bout you. All kind of stories are going round. One bunch says you burnt down old Henrys house and then killed youself by burning down your place. Thats what the laws are saying. Theres another story tho that you burned down Henrys place and then some of his hired help killed you and burned your house to cover it up. I think thats the most repeated story and the one maybe more folks think is right. That story sounds like the kind a thing that might go on round here and I think thats why its so poplar. But quite a few folks think something else entire. They say old Henry had your house burned down and tried to killed you but you slipped away and burned down his house and then took off. For those folks, your the biggest hero since Pretty Boy Floyd. I'm proud to say I've stuck with that story the past few months. Course I was privy to some inside info. You was past out in the grass when I left that night so I never did think you burned up in the house. I was afeared those thugs had killed you and burned you up long with the house tho. When nobody heard nothing from you for so long, I admit I begun to have some douts. But I knew old Henrys place did not burn by itself so I never did give up on you. Speaking of your uncle Henry, I guess he bout had a cat fit when you slipped away. He had half the county out looking for you and they was combing ever chicken coop, outhouse and dry gulch all the way to Arkansas. Gossip has it he lost a big chunk of cash in the fire and the insurance company won't pay off. By the way, we got a new sheriff. Old Henry pushed Johnson so hard he got *kilt trying to catch up to you. Some people say old Henry had a knock down drag out with those little fellars that he talks to. Blamed them for his troubles. If'n it was anybody else round here, they'd be in the looney bin up to Vinita by now. But Henry greased a few palms and bought him a new house trailer and I guess he's still as onery as ever. Partner, I was shore tickled to get your letter. You come out smelling like roses. When you run, you shore keep running a long ways. I was thinking California or maybe even old Mexico, but I never thunk you would get so far off. I dont know what I will do for a drinking partner now that your gone. I shore would like to know the story of how you ever got from lying drunk in the yard to where you are now in that forin place on the other side of the world. Write me up the whole story would you? I got nothing to do all day here in the pokey and Im just bored spitless. I will try to keep this all to myself but Im flat just busting to tell it. That lake explanes a lot about what went on. Well, I am plum tuckered from all this writing and it is almost lights out time. Wish you was here. Ha Ha.*

Your bud,
Ed

In November the southern sun began to warm the land and Lonnie was glad he had taken Fernando's advice and had built the cabin where it would be shaded part of the day by a grove of *ombu* trees, a strange tall evergreen which looked more like a giant weed. The grass on the pampas started shooting up so fast you could almost see it grow and the horses began to fatten up. Most of the mares were carrying foals and those that were not were being bred to a fiery red roan stallion Lonnie had borrowed from a neighbor.

The local ranchers had been cool at first but they were rapidly accepting Lonnie even though he was an *Americano*. Cowboys from the states had been drifting down to the pampas and working on the big *estancias* for about eighty years but they were often just looking for an adventure and left after a few months. It was Fernando who convinced the locals that Lonnie was different, that he was there to stay. The pivotal point he made in talking with his fellow gauchos was that Lonnie loved horses in the same way the gauchos did, above all his other possessions. Fernando was viewed with respect in the gaucho brotherhood and his praise stood Lonnie in good esteem among the men and when the ranch owners in turn learned from them of Lonnie's ardor for horses, they began to look at him in a different way.

It was a time of anticipation and excitement for Lonnie and he did not reflect on the things Ed had said in his letter. He was too busy riding out among his mares, getting to know each of them personally, listening to the things they whispered, carried on the wind, smelling the rich pungent perfume of lush grass and horse sweat. But as time grew close for a resupply trip to town, Lonnie sat down and filled several pages of the old writing tablet.

>*Hey Ed,*
>
>   *It was real good to get your letter. I hope by the time you get this you will be a free man again. Things are going well here. You are pretty close about what happened just before I took off. I was passed out in the yard wen they set the house afire. I had all the guns out there but we shot up all the ammo so I was in a tight spot. Guess I'm real lucky to be alive. If I'd of been in the house, doubt I would have made it out as they were laying for me. When I made a run for the house, some bastard took a shot at me and didn't miss by much. When I got in I realized there wasn't a thing I could do about the fire. The house was too far gone. I grabbed up a few things and managed to slip out*

the back under the cover of the blowing smoke and made it to the barn. They must of figured I died in the fire. The bastards killed my dogs. That's how lowdown they were. I hid out in the barn the rest of the night thinking long and hard. The next morning, they were gone. I never even saw one of their faces, but I know who they were and who put em up to it. I just saddled up Buster and rode off. I guess you figured out some of what I did that day and it might be best not to put some of it in writing. I can say by that afternoon I was riding north on old Buster into Sequoyah County. I camped that night at Brushy Lake and it wasn't until I dismounted that I realized I'd gone all day without eating and just how tired and hungry I was. It might not of been too smart but I built up a fire and fried up some bacon and threw in a can of beans and used the bean can to boil water for coffee. That meal was one of the best I ever ate because I felt like my own man for the first time in a coon's age. I felt free of everything and it just made me want to put more distance behind me. I slept the next night on the pool table at Tuffy's County Line and old Tuffy was kind enough to feed me something. The next morning Buster and I kept moving north into the Cookson Hills. Indian summer was in full swing. Warm days and cool nights. We camped that night on the banks of a clear little creek and I had the beans and bacon supper again. The next day I wasn't paying close enough attention and we strayed off the trail and got lost. I tried to backtrack but an early fall rain came up that afternoon and we ended up camping under a rock overhang. Sometime during the night, coons got into the food stores and ate up everthing but the cans of beans. The next morning I decided the best idea would be to strike out to the east until I hit the river and follow it north. It was tough going that day, through dense brush, up and down the sides of rocky slopes and worst of all when we came to the river we were on a high bluff with no way to get down to it that I could find. I was hungry and tired and Buster was showing signs that he needed rest.

We camped on the bluff and it started raining again that night and kept raining for two days. Food was about gone and we pushed on. Soaked to my drawers, I was so wet my skin wrinkled up all over and it was miserable cold and not a dry place to sleep. I got turned around and lost again and we blundered around in a cold, wet rain and on the second night I finished off the last of the beans.

The next morning the sun came out and I decided to just head west and try to find highway 82. It turned out to be a long walk and Buster began limping and I ended up leading him along at a slow pace. Buster was in pitiful shape by the end, hopping along on three legs and I believe he was suffering quite a bit. The rain and the long walk was bad on my leg and by the end we were both just barely able to keep going. On the second day, I heard the sound of cars going down the road and we worked our way out to the highway. I stopped at a bait shop and called Leonard and waited in the edge of the woods and he came with his horse trailer and hauled us out of there and back to his house. I spend a few days resting up there eating his wife's good cooking. After I recovered a little Leonard drove me over to Tahlequah and we shopped around some and I bought a clunky old pickup for $200. It was a hard decision, but I had to say goodbye to Buster. I left him with Leonard where I knew he would be well taken care of, but I drove away feeling like I'd lost my last friend in the world. If you get a chance when you get out, take him a measure of the best oats you can find and some apples.

That old truck wasn't worth what I paid for it and didn't get me very far. It threw a rod outside Huntsville, Texas and

I left it on the side of the road. I hitched into town and found the bus station and bought a ticket south to the border. Carrying around two rifles with me brought a lot of stares so while I was waiting for my bus I found a gun shop and sold the saddle gun and the twenty-two but I kept the old Colt Peacemaker and still have it. The next day I crossed into old Mexico and got another bus to Monterey. I had thoughts of staying a while or maybe even settling down somewhere below the border but I soon figured out that northern Mexico is nothing but a huge desert. I stopped off for a couple of days in Monterey and moped around, wondering what the mex jails were like, then got on another bus for Mexico City. Talk about an anthill. I only spent one night there and there were cars honking and people hollering all night long and I did not get much sleep until I got back on the bus. Now I was in the mountains, up among the clouds, but I still had not seen any place that looked like land good enough to farm or ranch so I just kept going.

I couple of days later we crossed over into Guatemala and we were in the jungle and then I rode on through a bunch of little countries and I don't even think I could tell you the name of all of them but after a few days I got off the bus in Panama City. That ride is just all kind of scrambled up in my brain, and the only thing I remember is that I was convinced we were going to fly off a narrow road and take a thousand foot drop and nobody would ever know what happened to me. After days of the scariest bus ride you can imagine I was back on American soil in the canal zone and that made me nervous so after just a couple of days I booked passage on a little ship for Buenos Aires. We were not out of the canal an hour before I began puking my guts out and I spent most of the time on that ship in bed in my cabin.

When we finally got there I was just glad to be back on solid ground again. I spent a few days just walking around the city. I would not want to live there but it is as pretty a town as I have seen, wide streets and buildings with arched doors and windows all over the place and lot of palm trees. There are many outdoor cafes, one on almost every corner and the street is filled with the smell of roasting coffee beans and smoked beef. I was lonesome as hell though and felt out of place and I didn't know any Spanish so I couldn't talk to anybody. I spent my days walking around and feeling sorry for myself and cussing myself for a fool. It was my low point and I just about turned tail and headed back to the states. I realized I was chasing a dream, a dream I might not be able to pull off. I was there about two weeks feeling doubtful about the whole thing.

Then one day I was walking down the street and I heard the sound of English being spoke. It was funny sounding English but I didn't care. It was coming from a family walking in front of me. I followed along for a while and then I worked up the nerve to talk to them. Turned out they were from the Welsh colony in the southern part of the country and they had lived there all their life. They were on vacation and were on their way out to dinner and invited me to come along. I did and it was the break I needed to turn things around.

That dinner made all the difference. The food was good but the talk is what saved me. I heard about the pampas, the big ranches there, the gauchos. I learned the difference between the wet and dry pampas, which one was good for ranching, which one wasn't. The most important thing I found out was that the government was in the land business and I might be able to buy a tract from them. I guess I made my first friends here that night. They invited me to come down and see them at their place way down south. I hope to get down there one of these days.

The next day I went to the government land office and I had to wait in line several hours just to look over what they had for sale. There was plenty being offered. I spent the next couple of weeks splitting my time between riding the rails down to the pampas to scout out the land and standing in lines in the government land office. It was early spring and the land was greening up, a thick carpet of grass already growing. Almost at first sight I knew I could live here.

I spent a few more days at the land office when I went back to Buenos Aires and I thought I was never going to get through all the paperwork. Just about the time I thought I was about to close a deal, some clerk would bring up something new, some problem and I'd have to go to the back of the line again. I finely figured it out. Argentina is a lot like LeFlore County. The next time a problem came up, I slipped the clerk a hundred bucks American money and my troubles disappeared. I bought the land and then I checked out of my hotel and took the train back and the first thing I did when I got here was to buy me a good horse.

That's how I got here, old bud. Looking back it was almost too easy and truth be known I only wish I would of done it sooner. What's going on back there? Don't go spreading any of this around. Just let folks think I've gone to my reward because, actually, I really have. Adios.

Your old bud,
Lonnie

In December summer came to the pampas and the land shimmered and danced in the distance like the heat was liquid glass poured down. He missed things then, like ice, and fans and cool spring water. And he began to miss other things not connected with summer, his friend, his child, his old horse, and even, though it was hard to admit, his homeland. Some nights he lay in his new cabin unable to keep his mind from drifting back. Cheeseburgers and fries, pecan pie, the old pickup rolling down a back road, football games, the cool escape of the picture show, the whistle of the Kansas City Southern locomotive, the yeasty smell of a beer joint, all haunted him like ghosts from a past life. Despite himself, his thoughts sometimes returned to Ramona.

He retreated to the yard and slept outside under the stars and in the evening Fernando played his *payadore* songs, singing lyrics he had written about his life on the open range. The melodies to accompany were classical flamenco measures infused with notes from the starkness and vastness of the landscape and there was a loneliness there that made him feel insignificant the same way a sky full of stars can overwhelm the mind and make one wonder if anything really matters.

He fought the feelings of isolation and desolation by spending all day in the saddle riding out among the swelling mares, trying to wear himself out so that sleep would come easily and phantoms from his past would not visit his nights.

A few days before Christmas he drove the team to town to restock, buy some Christmas presents and just get away for a day or two. He visited the outdoor market and found a good gift for Homer, a prancing horse carved from a block of dark wood. After some consideration he bought Ed a good bottle of Chilean wine and some of the strong tobacco Fernando favored. For Leonard he purchased a new bridle and a rainbow colored horse blanket. And for Clay, he bought a pair of fine hand-tooled boots. For Fernando, he selected a new saddle in the gaucho style, padded up with rags, as well as a large tin of *hierba mate*. After finishing his shopping he picked up his mail.

The envelope had a postmark that was two months old and the letter had been posted in TULSA, OK. When he opened the envelope the first thing to slide out was a photo of Clay standing on a beach with a wave breaking around his cowboy boots. On the flip side of the photo he had written, *"Me getting my feet wet in the Pacific Ocean near San Fran."* There was a sheaf of three letters under the photo, the top one in Clay's schoolboy scrawl.

> *Dear Dad,*
> *Your letter caught up with me here in Tulsa. I came back in time to start the new school year. California was a great place to visit and I'm glad I went out there but I found out it's not all sunshine and pretty girls. School is pretty boring but I'm going to try to stick it out. I would like to come spend the summer with you if I can find a way to get down there. Mom has already said it's okay with her. Hope you don't mind but I told her about your letter. She'd already seen the foreign stamps anyway and had pretty much figured it all out. Not much has changed here, still the same old place, same old people. Guess you had yourself an adventure, huh? I think you surprised some people. Don't worry about losing the old homeplace. Your new place sounds better anyway. Can't wait to see it. Write me and tell me all about it. Glad to know you are fine and doing well. I think about you all the time. I'm saving my money up to buy me a horse when I come down. See if you can find me a good one. I'll write again soon.*
> *Love, Clay*

He recognized the simple but pretty handwriting of the second letter as Janeen's.

> *Hi Lonnie,*
> *Well, aren't you a wild one. You gave me a good scare. Here I was all flustered over Clay when I guess you were the one*

I should have been worried about. I'm glad it's all turned out all right for you. I don't blame you for what you did and neither does Larry. That old coot had it coming. Did you have to go so far away? I thought outlaws just went down to Mexico and hid from the law there. I can tell Clay misses you even though he'd never say a thing to me about it. He was so happy to get your letter. I saw tears in his eyes. He's got his heart set on coming to see you next summer and I guess it's alright with me. Lonnie, I wish you well and I hope you are happy now. It's too bad about Ramona. I thought you two were going to get together. I heard she is getting married soon. I'm sure you will find someone, maybe one of those nice pretty senoritas down there. It's really none of my business what you do but I am thinking good thoughts for you.

Janeen

The third letter was typed on a letterhead from Larry Looper Enterprises, Inc. It was on stiff white watermarked paper and had been sharply creased into thirds.

Dear Cousin,

I'm sure this letter is unexpected and maybe even unwelcome but there are a few family matters that need to be settled and this is the best way I can find to handle them.

I don't know if you've heard but dad passed away a few weeks back. I've been trying to settle his business affairs the best I can under the circumstances. I also don't know if you knew about plans by the U.S. Army Corps of Engineers to dam up the river and form a big lake in the area of your family's old home.

Last week I accepted an offer of $22,500.00 from the Corps for your family's land. I believe the proceeds from the sale rightly belong to you.

I have deducted the $5,000.00 you have received previously and you will find a bank draft in your name for $17,500.00 at the Western Union office in Buenos Aires.

I know this will not make up for the injustice you have suffered in this matter. I believe there is nothing that could.

Even though you may not believe me, I wish you success in your new venture.

Sincerely,

Larry Looper

On Christmas Eve Lonnie and Fernando sat cross-legged in the yard and watched the crescent moon rise over the pampas golden and curved into the shape of a bull's horns. It was one of those clear mid-summer nights when there are so many stars out they appear to swarm together into one dazzling haze of points. The starlight streamed down so bright that you could see miles across the pampas and they could sit there and watch the mares half-heartedly grazing a half mile off.

They were finishing off a supper of steak empanadas and drinking cervezas. Several beers were chilling in a bucket of ice. The ice had been hauled out from town special for the occasion, and Fernando was thoughtfully pulling at a cooled brew for the first time, not sure what to think of drinking it that way. In his improved Spanish, Lonnie was urging him on and offering shots from a bottle of good American bourbon.

After supper Lonnie presented Fernando with the new saddle and the old man's eyes widened in surprise and delight.

"*Me siento ahora a las mil maravillas.*"

His gift to Lonnie was a wide leather belt studded with Argentine coins much like the one he wore.

"*Ahora tu es un gaucho en verdad.*"

They lay on their backs late into the night watching the moon cross the field of stars and listening to the silky sound of the wind sieving through the fields. The moon was directly over them by the time the whiskey relaxed them into sleep.

Clay arrived early in June and Lonnie had a beautiful palomino waiting in the corral for him. They rode out together every day among the bulging mares and Clay took to the life as if he were born to it. He slept out in the yard with Fernando and in his broken Spanish pestered the old man to teach him the gaucho tricks, which astounded and delighted him. He adopted gaucho dress, donning the loose trousers, *bombachos*, the poncho and even the red sash at the waist. When the summer began to cool to lukewarm, Clay boarded a big PanAm plane and flew home, but it was just for a visit. He gathered up his things and flew back a month later to take up permanent residence.

It was in September, close to a year after Lonnie arrived in country that the first colt was born, a little red roan, which wobbled onto its legs minutes after leaving the womb. In the days that followed, the mares foaled one beautiful small horse after another and they thrived and soon began cropping the tender spring grass. Lonnie rode among the remuda and admired the colts like a proud father with thirty new children.

The three men and the horses lived in contentment. The wind had weathered his face and the sun tanned his hide like a piece of leather until his eyes showed white and brilliant against the darkness of his face. He let his dark hair grow until it fell onto his collar and then onto his shoulders.

"*Muy guapo*," Fernando teased him. He climbed out of bed

eager to greet each new day and he eased under the covers every night anticipating the next and the days flowed away in a golden haze.

It was the season of his life, a time that all things past dropped away for good, like an old wound, which has finally healed, and he was at peace with the past like a country over the horizon he had once visited briefly long ago.

Printed in the United States
65451LVS00007B/16-18